Off the Wall

a novella by

Kari Wergeland

Finishing Line Press
Georgetown, Kentucky

Off the Wall

ACKNOWLEDGMENTS

I offer my gratitude for the Big Picture Manuscript Workshop taught by
David Ulin and Amy Wallen. I would also like to thank my warmhearted
friend, Patricia Santana, for suggesting I take this workshop and for her keen
proofreading eye.

Publisher: Leah Huete de Maines
Editor: Christen Kincaid
Cover Art: Timothy Pagaard
Author Photo: Valeria Tutrinoli
Cover Design: Timothy Pagaard

Order online: www.finishinglinepress.com
              also available on amazon.com

Author inquiries and mail orders:
Finishing Line Press
P. O. Box 1626
Georgetown, Kentucky 40324
U. S. A.

Table of Contents

The Diner

A few tables in the old diner had a view of the harbor where the ferry from Seattle docked. What made people smile were the dollar bills. Some displayed colorful notes written in a moment of spontaneity. *Peace. Dan. See Birds rock!* Someone—once upon a time—had started this trend, tacking one dollar on the wall. Now there had to be damn near two thousand decorating the place.

The diner served burgers, fish and chips, and a few specialty items, like the chicken quesadilla. Sadie knew them all by heart. She'd been working there since she turned sixteen, two years to this day. Her aunt and uncle—they took her in after her mother died of a heroin overdose—were quick to point out how lucky she was to have a job at her age—on the island—given the job market these days. She had experience, so she probably wouldn't starve. *No matter how bad your grades are.*

Last time she checked, her GPA hovered at around 2.7. Mr. Colsten, the guidance counselor, recently tackled her in the hallway to report she would graduate on time if she could finish her last two quarters with a C average or better.

She flipped her blonde bangs back, thinking about how Aunt Linny liked to label her hair in a way that made it sound dirty. *Dishwater.* Linny and Leonard. Leonard was her uncle. Those two loved pointing out how cute their names sounded next to each other. She once considered dyeing her hair red, but she'd become a penny pincher since she'd started this job. That meant she worked hard to stay away from hair dye, lipstick, all the stuff she loved. She stayed away from cigarettes, too—though smoking tempted her. The fact she boasted her own savings account with her own debit card had been no small feat. Leonard helped her get it, and when Linny found out, an outburst ensued.

"It's Sadie's money," Leonard insisted.

"It'll burn a hole in her pocket."

"Let her learn from her mistakes."

"Her mother didn't."

"Her father was worse," he retorted.

Sadie's mother had been Uncle Leonard's sister. Her father… Nobody knew where her father was.

"You know Cecilia flashed her be-hind to pay for heroin. That or she stole something," Aunt Linny scoffed.

"Linny, please! Sadie might hear you."

A momentary truce had been formed over the debit card. Yet she knew her aunt was looking for an excuse to take it away. "If I catch you using…"

Linny was always freaking. Certain Sadie would get tangled up in drugs. That was the example Sadie's mother had set, Linny reasoned out loud. More than once.

Sadie never suggested she might have done her own thinking about stuff. She never said her mother's life had ruined any taste she might have had for getting high. Her mother's life was the reason why Linny and Leonard were her official guardians. They were stuffy people with big ass jobs in Seattle.

No, Sadie never bothered to tell them she barely touched the money she earned each month, though Leonard probably knew. His name was on the account. At least it wasn't hers! Leonard probably knew she had nearly $15,000 saved. Now that she was finally eighteen, one of the first things she planned to do was get his name off. She was damn proud of her stash, but she was no fool. $15,000 wouldn't last long if she tried to live on her own.

That guidance counselor was breathing down her neck, though. Mr. Colsten insisted she could attend a community college on financial aid. He said this after she mentioned how her aunt and uncle weren't going to pay for anything. The counselor almost had her convinced. She could go to college, with her grades. She could start over in a new school, show everyone how smart she really was. Mr. Colsten told her all of that, which had been news to her, based on what her aunt always said. "Sadie, there's no way in hell any college will take you now!"

But then the counselor told her Linny and Leonard would have to hand over a copy of their tax return when she filled out the FAFSA. Oh man! It wasn't even worth asking.

A week ago, Linny made this big deal out of announcing how Sadie could plan on paying rent once she turned eighteen. She'd bitten right back "I've got plans!" That had been a lie—at the time.

"How do you think you're going to find a good job, huh? With your grades. Do you even know what rents are?" Linny was a fading beauty, but the smile that followed wasn't pretty. "If you don't stick around and keep yourself clean, you're going to end up like your mother."

"Her order is ready!" Bev shouted, causing Sadie to spin and notice the food piling up on the little counter that served as the base of a small rectangular hole in the wall.

She nodded at her plump boss and zipped over to reach for the basket of fish and chips, which she toted to Margot. Margot was Linny and Leonard's financial planner. She had dark brown curly hair and red glasses. She lived on the island with her husband, but worked in Seattle, like most people.

"Looks tasty," Margot exclaimed, as Sadie set the food down. The financial planner was always upbeat in her presence. Sadie decided this was because Margot considered her "at risk." During some session focused on Linny and Leonard's financial future, she overheard Margot complimenting her aunt for taking on a child in need.

"Sadie is at risk," Linny had countered.

She was frowning at the memory when Margot brought her back to the present. "Thanks, Sadie."

Startled, she glanced at the financial planner, feeling a streak of discomfort shooting through her gut. "Oh sure," she replied, adjusting her expression to aim for good customer service in the way Bev had taught. "Can I get you anything else?"

Margot eyed her appraisingly. "Linny tells me you've decided against applying for college."

Oh man!

"She says you'll be looking for more work, come summer."

"Ketchup?"

Margot shook her head. The financial planner started to say something else, but Sadie pretended not to notice as she turned and raced back to the hole in the wall. She leaned on the little counter and poked her head through to see how Bev was doing with the pile of orders. "Bev... Anything else?"

"Don't forget our little celebration," Bev grinned. Her boss had this way of shooting dimples at people. "After this dive closes, I mean."

Sadie laughed. Bev and her husband, Nate, owned "this dive." They'd built the business together. "We're a great team!" Bev always boasted, before launching into her tale about how they got started. From what Sadie understood, the couple had begun with almost nothing. Now they were considered a pair of pillars on the island. They were involved in a bunch of community groups that Bev said ate up way too much time. But they wanted to pitch in. "It's important, Sadie," Bev said one time.

So it was Thursday, she calculated. That meant they'd be eating stale fries at 10:30 pm. *What the hell.* She could fit it in. Bev didn't know it was her last day. She had a Hallmark card all ready, one that explained the basics. *I'm eighteen now, and I need to find my own way. Thanks for being the best boss ever!* She'd leave it somewhere in the diner before she took off. Her fingers were crossed she'd never be back. She prayed her plan was rock solid.

And she did have a plan.

After Linny informed her about the impending rent payments, Sadie decided it was bullshit! Her friends weren't paying any rent. She came up with her own idea and jumped on her bike, pedaling to the library. Once she was seated before an internet terminal, she went straight to Amtrak. As she placed the reservation, she willed her debit card to work on the library computer. She'd wanted to leave on her birthday, but as she plugged in the departure date, Bev's invitation spun through her head. *Then let's you and me get together...*

Bev had tried to get Sadie to take her birthday off, but she'd shaken her head at that one. She hated missing any opportunity to earn money. She was piling up money, right and left. She'd become obsessive about her stash, putting her arms around it and holding on tight. She was glad she'd decided to work on her birthday. Every little bit helped. The celebration with Bev would be a great way for her to say goodbye without Bev knowing it.

As the night deepened and people began leaving, she and Bev mopped and wiped everything down. When the door was locked, her boss brought out two plates.

"You sit," Bev motioned. "I've got a little something in the back! Her boss returned with a couple of Redhooks and a wrapped present. "This place is closed, so they can't say anything about me serving someone underage. Besides, this is a family celebration. A special one, given how you are now an official adult." Bev opened the two beers and handed one over. "Cheers, Baby!"

"Thanks," Sadie said bashfully as they clinked bottles.

She rarely had time to party, but she'd done it a time or two. Hell, her and Bev had done this before, stale fries and all.

"You still thinking South Seattle?" Bev asked.

She knew her boss meant the community college. "I do have some peeps there," she replied, as if South Seattle College was her destiny. She didn't have the heart to tell her there was no way in hell she was going to that school now. Best not to give away her plan.

"Let's see the new driver's license."

She'd just passed her driver's test. Leonard helped her get it because he thought she could start running some errands. He and Linny put in such long hours in Seattle.

Whatever.

"Just a sec, Bev." She made her way to the tiny workroom and grabbed her bag. "You gotta see this," she exclaimed, settling back into her chair. "My mug isn't bad."

"Give it," Bev demanded in that perky way of hers, though her face did look tired. Bev's thinning brown hair was damp where it touched her skin.

Sadie opened her wallet, and there it was, all official. Her first driver's license, nestled behind a clear plastic window. "See?"

"Nice!" Bev whistled. "You'll be living with that one a while."

Before she shoved her wallet back into her purse, Sadie glanced at the little pockets where her other cards were stored. She couldn't believe this. "Shit!"

"What?"

"Somebody fucking stole it!"

"What?"

"My debit card!"

"Not here Sadie."

"Someone sure as hell did!"

"Did you look through all the compartments—your bag?"

She rifled through her stuff more thoroughly, fighting a sensation that could easily become tears. The Coast Starlight departed at 9:35 tomorrow morning. She didn't have time to get a new card. What if someone already cleaned her out? What if her aunt did it? Linny wasn't beyond pulling shit like this.

"That fucking bitch!"

"Anything?" Bev looked at Sadie with her usual equanimity. More than once, she'd watched Bev respond in this way to certain customers. Bev was pure cool-calm.

"Not a fucking thing!" She caught her boss's expression. "Sorry about the swearing. It's just…"

Bev produced a phone. "Call now."

"What?"

"Report the card lost. Now! Then your funds will be safe."

"If someone hasn't fucking taken them."

"Let me do it," Bev said, holding out her hand. "You're too upset. Someone can probably tell us what your balance is."

Bev made regular deposits into Sadie's account, so she knew which bank to call. Her boss held the phone to her ear, and then she touched a number. She listened once more. Then she touched another number. "Here," she said. "Someone will be with you in a moment. You can report the card lost AND ask about your balance. All right?"

"OK," Sadie breathed, feeling a little better, though not much.

More relief coursed through her when she learned the money was still there. She told the woman on the line to kill the card. That part was easy. Then the woman asked if her address was still good. "We can mail you a new one right away."

Sadie lowered the phone. "Um, excuse me, Bev. Could I have some privacy?"

"Sure…" Her boss jumped up and headed for the kitchen.

She spoke softly into the phone. "Do you have any branches in San Diego?" Sadie knew they did because she'd tried to think of everything. She nattered at the woman, as fast as she could, because she didn't want Bev to hear. She was moving to San Diego. She didn't have her new address just yet. She'd find a good branch in San Diego and update everything once she got settled. The woman thought that would be just fine. "Thanks," Sadie finally said and clicked off the phone.

She moseyed into the kitchen to see if Bev needed help.

"Everything all right?" her boss asked.

She nodded, before reaching for some silverware.

"No way, Lady. This is your birthday. You go back out there and sit." Bev grasped the handle of the deep fryer to raise it a foot, before setting it back down with a bang. "These fries are too cold. Let's skip 'em. I'll heat up some chowder, and I've got fresh bread."

She hovered till Bev dismissed the air between them with one hand. "Young lady… You get on out there."

This changed everything, she thought as she took her seat. This mess with the card. Because she needed it now—or tomorrow, anyway. She needed money for meals, money to get a hotel. Who knew what else? She had her ID, her social, a little cash, and the train ticket. She didn't have a cell phone. Her aunt and uncle were too cheap for that. Horrible though it was to be the only kid on the island without one, she'd never tried to spend her own money to keep up. She'd been counting on her debit card, though. It was the easiest way to pay for stuff. She really should head home and try and figure this out. But Bev had always been good to her. Sadie would stay for the party.

The beer helped her relax. She was dying to tell her boss about the trip. She was moving to San Diego. San Diego! She wanted to tell Bev about the beaches, the sunshine. But she bit it all back. She needed to get out of this place without anyone knowing where she was headed. If she told Bev one teensy-weensy detail, her boss would drag the rest out of her. She'd experienced Bev's tenacity more than once.

Bev brought out a tray with the chowder, some fresh bread, and two pieces of apple pie. They sat facing each other over the fifties-style linoleum table, sipping and slurping—munching. Her boss started cracking up at her own tale about her second to last customer of the night—who was probably a tourist. He'd ordered two burgers before pinching her butt. Bev fought back by grabbing some leftover fries from another table. They were all bloody due to the ketchup squirted across the top. Anyway, she placed the basket in front of this guy, and then she proceeded to tell him—in that calm voice of hers—that she had a husband. She flashed her diamond ring. And maybe he'd prefer some French fried potatoes. And then the guy actually ate a few. Moments later, the guy pulled a dollar bill off the wall and tried to stuff it into her pants. That's when Bev told him to get out.

And that was when Sadie realized how she could get out of her debit card mess. That and come away with some extra money for the hotel and whatever else she needed to tide her over until she could get to the bank.

"Um… Excuse me, Bev. I gotta use the head."

"We should probably wrap this up…"

"It was cool of you to do this." She gestured at the spoils on the table, feeling a twinge of love.

When Bev shooed her away, she shot into the bathroom, where she undid the latch on the window, hoping, hoping Bev would miss it when she closed up. She knew Bev didn't think she'd take anything. So… *Not here, Sadie.* That thought hit her hard. And she wouldn't have, she insisted to herself, as guilty feelings prodded and poked. Bev wasn't planning to ever use this money… It was decoration. So maybe two hundred dollars? She didn't want to travel without enough cash.

On Rick Steves, Rick always said the first thing he did when he arrived at his destination was head for an ATM machine. That was what she'd been planning, only now she didn't have her debit card. She couldn't leave the island, only to wander the streets like a homeless girl. She'd been counting on plastic. She'd worked hard for this. If only she'd withdrawn more cash yesterday. She had about $100 stashed in her room at Leonard and Linny's. $100 would surely cover her first night in a cheap hotel, but then what would she eat? She didn't want to starve during the forty-hour train ride. And she didn't have time to go into her bank before the Coast Starlight rolled away from Seattle.

She left the bathroom, trying not to stare at the dollar bills all around the room. If she did this right, maybe Bev wouldn't even notice.

Sidling up to the hole in the wall, she asked, "Bev… What can I help you with?"

"I think we're good." Bev slapped her hands together.

Sadie watched to see if Bev would check the head one last time, but her boss moved to the register and began fiddling with a pile of receipts. One by one, Bev stuck them through a single spike. "That bastard never paid!" she fumed.

Sadie made sympathetic noises as she followed her boss out the door.

They stood together on the pavement in front of the darkened diner, and Bev told Sadie to sleep well, as she always did, which made her feel teary-eyed, because who knew when they'd see each other again? Bev had no idea this was a serious goodbye.

"Bye Bev."

She tried to look normal as she waved and turned toward her battered bicycle. But she wanted to bawl. She could hear her boss's footsteps cross the parking lot—she heard Bev's keys jingling, the sound of seagulls, the car door shutting tight. The outside air pressed dampness into her skin, though it wasn't raining.

As soon as Bev drove away, she relocked her bike and looked toward the shadows. Two street lamps stood on either side of the diner, but the back of the restaurant was dark. A small forest bordered the pavement behind the building, black conifers personified by the night. All in her mind, of course.

The bathroom window wasn't difficult to open from the outside, and this calmed her. She tossed her bag through. It was harder to hoist her compact body into the darkened room. She figured she'd have several bruises and a scrape by the time she was through.

Once she felt safe in the bathroom, she lowered the window, so it would look right from the outside. She headed into the eating area, which was eerie now and still stinky from all the frying, not to mention the cleaning products. The dollar bills came off sinister. They were dark green pieces of paper cluttering up the walls. Bev should go for a different design scheme, she decided, as she tugged at a dollar bill.

She was selective, searching for bills with no writing on them, stuffing each one into her bag. She tried not to take too many from any one location—she used a chair to reach the higher ones. As she went about her work, scraping the chair across the floor to different places, every night noise got to her, every imagined spy. She'd look around the room, before reaching for another dollar, certain someone would figure out what she was up to, convinced she'd be nabbed with the stolen money in her purse. Then there would be hell to pay.

Bev!

Sadie's guilt had this way of bellowing. She didn't want her boss to know she was doing this. Because Bev believed in her.

When she'd taken enough money, she scanned the room one final time, trying to convince herself she'd chosen carefully. It didn't look too different. *Did it?*

Flipping her hair back, she headed for the bathroom. The job was done. *Done!* Maybe Bev would figure out what happened. Maybe she wouldn't. If she did, Linny would spout off about how Sadie was a little thief. Her aunt would sneer about how she knew Sadie would become just like her mother.

She inched the small window up so she could scoot back through, and another thought made her freeze. *The card!* She'd planned to leave it for Bev. She'd wanted to give her boss a real goodbye, which was why she'd bought the card. She reached for her bag and rummaged through the crumpled bills until her fingers touched the white envelope. But then her shoulders turned rock solid around her own spinning thoughts. She forced herself to stand straight as she felt her entire being deflate. The card wouldn't be welcome now that she'd helped herself.

She hated this! But she left the card in her bag, zipping it tight. She opened the window all the way and tossed her bag to the ground before sliding out of the restaurant. Steady on her feet, her eyes darted around the empty parking lot. No one there but the unforgiving forest. She turned to shut the window to keep out other thieves. Then she traipsed over to the bike rack, where her bicycle was the lone occupant.

Pedaling down the street to the neighborhood where Linny and Leonard lived, she inhaled a couple of times. She had a ways to go before she was free.

The Coast Starlight

When she walked into the big ass house, Sadie found Linny lounging on the sofa. Her aunt clicked off the television. "You're late!"

She bit back what she wanted to say about being an adult now that she was eighteen. It was her birthday, and no one in this fucking house had even noticed! The weight of her bag felt heavy against her hip as she remembered the debit card. Fury arced all over again. She wanted to lay into her aunt about the card. She reined herself in with all the force she could muster. She didn't need a fight right now. She didn't want Linny to become suspicious.

"Bev wanted to celebrate my birthday," she explained, trying to make her words come off smooth.

Linny's expression was invasive, but she didn't press. "Leonard and I plan to take you to dinner tomorrow night."

"That's cool," she nodded. By then she'd be gone.

"I need you to drive me to the ferry tomorrow," Linny added tersely.

She tried to make her shrug look normal. "Sure."

She was already their chauffeur, she thought bitterly. Yet the answer earned her a dismissal for the night. She found the stairs and padded up to her room. After she slid inside, she checked the door, making sure it was shut tight before she turned and spotted a white envelope on her pillow. Her name was written across the front in Leonard's handwriting. It contained a fifty-dollar gift certificate for Verizon. *Toward your new phone! I'll put you on the family plan. Love Uncle Leonard and Aunt Linny.*

Definitely his doing, she thought, as she pushed the closet door open.

She pulled a pile of laundry off her mid-sized backpack and tossed it to the other side of the large closet, covering the shoes she wouldn't be taking. Her pack was already fat with her essentials. She'd gone over Linny's Rick Steves guide twice as she selected stuff for the trip. Unzipping a compartment on the outside of the pack, she tucked the Verizon gift certificate into one pocket, wondering if she could use it in San Diego. The phone part wasn't all that expensive, she decided. It was the service that costed.

Readying herself for bed, she tried not to fret about how tomorrow would go. Once she was under the covers, she arranged her pillows the way she liked and willed herself to relax so she could sleep.

It was still dark when she opened her eyes, only to fixate on her debit card all over again. She glanced at her clock. 3:17. Maybe it was in Linny's purse! She threw back her covers and tiptoed down the stairs to the living room. The purse rested on a side table. She searched Linny's wallet, feeling her anger arc, but did not find the card.

Damn!

Green edges caught her attention. It had never occurred to her to steal from this woman. Now she wasn't sure why. Her aunt didn't give her anything. Her uncle came through—sometimes—like the gift certificate—but Aunt Linny was a pain! Sadie slipped the money out and counted forty-seven dollars. Back in her room, she stuffed the cash into the money belt she'd purchased from a travel store in downtown Seattle. This was after she'd watched a Rick Steves video on avoiding theft.

She got back under the covers, but sleep was hopeless. She stared up at the dark ceiling. She stared toward the window. She stared at the illuminated numbers on the clock that sat on her nightstand. She began to dream without realizing she was dreaming. She was still in her bed near moonbeams as her mind played a story with characters she didn't recognize until the alarm sounded. Loud! She already felt jumpy.

Dressing carefully—jeans, running shoes, a warm sweater, and the money belt—she tried to think of everything. She tugged a knit hat over her head and wrapped a scarf around her neck. She pulled on a bulky rain jacket and put the hood up after glancing at the rain-streaked window. Not a moonbeam to be seen. She reached for the cheap reading glasses she recently purchased because she never wore glasses, and she didn't want people to recognize her at the ferry dock. *OK. Well…*

She picked up the midsized pack that would be her life until she decided what to do. She ran her arms through the straps, adjusting everything so the pack rode well against her back.

It was still dark when she sneaked outside to find the old bicycle hidden between two bushes near the garage. She pedaled through the light rain toward the ferry dock, the little drops cool against her cheeks.

Breathing in the briny air, she ditched the bike on a side street and padded to the covered area where the walk-ons waited. This was the free direction, which eliminated the potentially difficult step of having to buy a ticket. On the island, everyone knew everyone. She was trying not to leave a trail for Linny and Leonard to follow.

She figured they couldn't do anything to her now that she was eighteen, but Linny and Leonard had this way of forcing her to be their little helper—their cheap labor. Like they had this gardener who came twice a month. But Sadie was expected to keep the yards looking good between his work sessions. And last week they held a dinner party for this family they'd known forever. The daughter, Geena, seemed to like her pretty well. Sadie had looked forward to catching up. But then

Linny made her work practically the whole time. Like they were all sitting at the table, and Linny said, "Geena, would you prefer juice to milk? I forgot about your lactic acid intolerance." When Geena nodded, Linny looked pointedly at Sadie, who was expected to get up and serve her classmate.

Yes, she was their little helper. This was what she wasn't: their child.

She found her place in line where she could open a window on the side of the covered ramp and look out over the darkened harbor dotted with lights. She did this to avoid Margot, the financial planner, who'd queued up behind her. Margot was about seven people back. Sadie would have to see where on the boat the financial planner sat her butt down so she could be sure and sit somewhere else.

Finally, the line of walk-ons streamed forward, as cars and bicycles below rolled onto the ferry, rhythmically accelerating and bumping, honking occasionally. When Sadie was onboard, she stepped to one side and turned toward a rain-spattered window, just catching the back of Margot as the woman pushed her way across the boat. Sadie found a spot in the rear, scooching down a long vinyl seat that came with a table. Moments later, a couple she did not know claimed the seat across from her. A relief!

The woman caught her eye and smiled. Sadie smiled back. She smiled at the guy. The couple turned in unison to stare out the rain-speckled window. It was blue-dark, hard to see much, though ripples of the sound glinted light in places. She looked around to scrutinize other sleepy-eyed passengers waiting to cross the sound. She didn't notice anyone she knew.

Patting the top of her snug jeans, she thought about the money belt beneath. More bills had been stuffed into a wallet inside her pack because she couldn't get all those singles into the belt. She rummaged through an outside pocket of her pack and pulled out her latest romance novel. She pretended to read because she couldn't concentrate.

As the boat chugged forward, she would glance up at the window every so often to see how close they were to the Seattle skyline, all lit up in the dark of the morning. The boat glided closer, and the herd of lighted skyscrapers seemed to grow before her eyes.

Once the ferry docked, a bunch of people converged into position for quick disembarking, though it always took the ferry workers a while to get a ramp to the boat. She looked around to make sure Margot was well ahead of her. *There she was!*

When the passengers surged forward, Margot hit the off-ramp, clutching her briefcase, and clipping along with her head down as she pushed past people, bumping a few. Sadie breathed out and began to move. A Washington Ferries employee shouted, "Hi Sadie!" like he always did. She wasn't happy about his friendly wave, but she returned it, thinking this was better than acting weird. "Hi."

She smiled back at the nice man, before glancing over to where Margot might be hovering. But the financial planner had disappeared, probably to some place where money was being made.

She stayed with the crowd as she rushed across an even longer ramp leading from the ferry terminal to Seattle's downtown. She had a short walk to King Street Station, but she was breathing easier because Linny and Leonard couldn't stop her now. Though she wouldn't feel free until she felt the wheels of that train turning, the rhythmic rocking of the coach car. No, the Coast Starlight wouldn't depart for another three hours. She doubted Linny and Leonard would find her in the Amtrack waiting room, but…

She had one last unknown to fret over before she claimed her life. Boarding the train. Would they question her? She'd been told she looked younger than she was. But she couldn't be viewed as a runaway. She was eighteen! Free to go where she wanted. The train ticket was in her name, and she had ID. Even so, it felt like she was getting away with something.

Turning into the Starbucks near 1st, she stopped to study the menu. She decided to splurge on the sweetest, hottest drink. That and a breakfast sandwich. She rarely bought a treat like this, but today was special. She paid for her food and grabbed a table. As she ate her sandwich, she cheered for herself. She wished Bev could share this moment. She hoped Bev wouldn't hate her when she didn't show up for work on Saturday. Linny would no doubt trash-talk to the entire island about Sadie, her at-risk niece who was already ending up just like her mother.

Shaking this thought away, she remembered Bev's card. She'd stashed it with her essentials because she hadn't wanted Linny and Leonard to find it. She didn't want Linny and Leonard to have a clue as to why she was missing. She pulled it from her pack and looked it over. The envelope had a fuchsia heart sticker on the back. She'd lovingly written the word *Bev* neatly on the front. She had to get going!

On her way out the door, she dumped the card in the garbage. She began power walking along the sidewalk. First light was coming on—so were more sprinkles. Horns and rushing cars—people heading to work. She trod into Pioneer Square, the historic part of downtown, where vintage buildings were pointed out to tourists riding the Emerald City Trolley. Where college students got drunk on the weekends. Homeless people milled about. She clutched the straps of her backpack, feeling grateful for the money belt.

"Spare change?" "Spare change?" "God Bless." "Spare change?" "Have a nice day." She spotted the old clock tower jutting up from the King Street Station and closed in on the old brick building.

In the lobby, she claimed a seat, but she couldn't relax. She needed to calm down! She looked around. The waiting area was from the olden times. It was classy, though she'd heard there could be pimps in train stations. Pimps looking for runaways. But she wasn't running away. She was free to make her own decisions. Besides, the lobby was clean. It was filled with people like Linny and Leonard, Margot—people who rode the ferry between the island and Seattle.

Sometime later, a younger man materialized. He stopped before her. She tried not to stare as her eyes brushed over him. He was handsome, brown hair and big green eyes.

"Anyone sitting here?"

When she shook her head, he sat down next to her. For several heartbeats, she kept her gaze focused forward, hoping he would take the hint and keep out. She was afraid to be friendly, but she was also feeling the need for support. Finally, she inhaled and looked his way. "Are you on the 9:35? The Coast Starlight?"

He smiled wide. "I'm heading back to Eugene."

"Oh."

"I'm in school down there. Or I should be anyway. I had to take a quick break to help with something at home."

"You live in Seattle?"

"Mmm hmm. Green Lake. What about you?"

"Queen Anne," she nodded, lying through her teeth.

"Where are you headed?"

"Los Angeles." This was a lie, too.

"Are you in a sleeper?"

She shook her head.

His smile was kind. "Your rear is sure going to be sore by the time you get to L.A."

She was cracking up inside at his quip, but she kept her expression even. She wanted to trust him. She just wasn't sure it was a good idea.

"Really," he insisted. "The train is always late." He turned his head and looked at her. "You have amber eyes."

"Hazel."

An announcer cut in, and they both glanced at the clock. "We should probably get in line," he suggested.

This guy seemed real familiar with the routine.

As they stood in line, they continued chatting. His name was Ayden and his dad worked for Microsoft. His mother was a teacher. He had two younger sisters. When the line started to creep forward, she told him she was an only child. When he asked her where she'd gone to high school, she said Nathan Hale. She breathed a sigh of triumph when he told her he'd attended Garfield. He was believing her story!

They were finally called to the counter. Ayden went first. Sadie remained behind a line on the floor. She watched carefully as he showed his ticket to the man sitting beneath a sign that read, "Coach." Ayden turned back to her. "I'll wait for you near the train."

She felt squirmy and did not want anyone knowing anything, but she smiled at Ayden as if she didn't have a care in the world. She pulled out a copy of her eTicket and handed it to the clerk, feeling nervousness spike. *What if he asked questions?* But the man barely glanced at it. "You're in car six," he drawled. He wrote SAN on a slip of paper, before handing it to her. "Be sure to put this above your seat." He pointed to the door leading to the tracks, where the Coast Starlight gleamed.

She found Ayden standing near the train—he still had his ticket out. "I'm in car eight."

"I guess we can't sit together," she noted.

"We can in the Café Car."

"Oh."

"When do you get in?" he asked.

As she looked down at her ticket, she felt him peering over her shoulder.

"Um… After midnight. Tomorrow, that is."

"Your last name is Taube?"

She stared at him hard, and he held his hands up in surrender. "Relax. Nothing weird."

But she was kicking herself for letting him see the ticket. Did he also spot the SAN that stood for San Diego? She needed to think before she acted, or she'd have her ass up a shit creek before she got anywhere.

"It means dove," she said, trying to distract him. "Taube means dove."

"That's perfect!" When she smiled in response, he added, "I'll look for you in the Café Car. It's got better views."

"Maybe."

She did like him. Besides, she wasn't dating anyone. During her junior year, she'd become serious about a guy named Hunter. For the first time in a long while, she'd been content to be alive. The fact that Linny kept bitching about how he was going to get her pregnant never got to her. Hunter was real sweet—didn't pressure her or anything. They finally did it, but it was hard for them to find a private place. They hadn't done it often.

Then Hunter left the island to attend college back East. He said they were still together, but not long after that, she spotted him in a photo on Instagram, kissing someone else. She ran out of the house and headed for the woods to cry. She never let anyone see how he broke her heart. Though Bev figured it out. Bev was real gentle with her during that time. She sure wished she could talk to her boss about everything that had happened so far. But she was going to have to get over relying on Bev! Bev would be upset when she figured out what Sadie had taken off the wall.

A train worker near the door to car six gave her a seat number. She found the right one and placed the SAN card above it. Once she was situated with her precious backpack at her feet, her warmer layers stowed in the luggage rack above, she turned her nose toward the window and studied the station, bits of downtown Seattle. It was still drizzling, but the train felt warm and cozy.

Leave!

People kept streaming in, stopping to store luggage overhead before settling. Some continued down the aisle in the direction of the Café Car. She decided not to look for Ayden. Fortunately, no one claimed the seat next to hers, though someone might later. There were lots of stops ahead.

When the Coast Starlight finally swayed down the tracks, she found herself staring mindlessly at the Puget Sound, the wet-green-gray. She looked out over the places they stopped at, Tacoma, Olympia—Centralia. She'd been through these towns before.

They were just entering Vancouver when she noticed Ayden standing in the aisle. "Mind if I sit?"

"Sure. I mean, No."

He dropped into the seat next to hers. "See, we're already late. We were supposed to be in Portland at 1:50. It's nearly 2:10."

"I don't care when we get there. I like the scenery."

"I used to feel that way."

"You going to Oregon—or Oregon State?" She wanted him to do the talking.

"Oregon." He proceeded to tell her some more. He was an Environmental Studies major, but he didn't know what he would do once he graduated. "Maybe grad school and teaching." He cared about sustainability, wanted to contribute in some way. He told her a bunch of other stuff about environmental problems and his family, what he liked to do for fun.

"What are you majoring in?" he asked.

"I haven't decided," she answered, sucking in her breath. *He thought she was in college!*

He chuckled. "I know a lot of people majoring in Undeclared. What do you like to do?"

"I like organizing stuff, planning." In this attempt to make him believe she really was in college, she realized her answer was true. She'd enjoyed thinking about this trip, putting it together. All the little details. Getting it right.

"So… Business?"

"Maybe."

"Is your school in San Diego?" `

He did notice!

His eyes rolled up to the luggage rack. "It says San Diego."

"So?"

"You said you were going to L.A."

She held his gaze and her next line spun into her brain. "I was going to San Diego to see family, but then I decided to get off in L.A. first. Stay a few days. I'll get on another train to San Diego."

Ayden's expression intensified—the guy seemed to have lots of energy. She didn't want him contemplating her situation. More words came out in a rush. "That's because I want to check out Santa Monica College."

"Santa Monica College?"

She'd known about Santa Monica College, because Hunter's older brother ended up there after he bombed out of USC. That was how Hunter had put it.

"You're not in college yet?"

"I took a gap year."

"Why Santa Monica?"

My folks really want me to go to South Seattle, but Santa Monica sounds cool."

"You'd definitely get out of the rain!" he laughed.

She was enjoying her own creativity. "I haven't applied yet. I want to check it out first."

"You know anyone down there?"

"Leah," she nodded. "She goes to school there. She's going to pick me up at Union Station tomorrow night. Like I said, I was going to get off in San Diego, but last night Leah and I were talking on the phone. She begged me to stop in L.A. First. She said she'd show me around. I didn't bother changing my ticket."

The truth was, she was going to change trains at Union Station. Leah really lived in San Diego—Leah was attending San Diego State. She and Leah had sort of been tight in high school, so she figured Leah wouldn't mind the unexpected visit. Sadie planned to call her when she got there, but she didn't expect Leah to put her up or anything. She just wanted to learn the ropes.

"So, you're going to tour the Santa Monica campus?"

She nodded. "How long till we get to Eugene?"

Ayden pulled out his phone to check the time. "Probably three hours. Hungry?"

She tuned in to the hollowness in her gut, remembering she hadn't eaten since Starbucks.

"Tell you what," he said. "I'll treat you."

"You're on," she replied, even as she remembered Uncle Leonard's admonition. *Never accept money from strangers.* She grabbed her backpack and followed Ayden down the aisle—through some doors that opened into this in-between space linking cars. She loved the feeling of the train beneath her feet, the adventure of moving past the outside world. They continued traipsing by rows and rows of seats until they reached a car that was designed quite differently. It was set up with some tables, as well as some seats facing the windows.

"The snack bar is down here." Ayden motioned toward the stairs, and she followed him down the narrow steps.

Together, they looked over the menu. Sandwiches and pizza—chicken tenders.

"I almost made a reservation for lunch in the dining car," he pointed out. "Their food is much better."

She looked around at the candy bars and the drinks. She saw how she could order hot food, like pizza. "This is good." She pulled out her wallet.

He touched her arm. "Really, Sadie. It's on me." When she looked at him steadily, he added, "No strings."

"Thanks!" she answered brightly, shoving the wallet back into her pack. Ayden was the nicest person she'd dealt with in a while.

He ordered the Garden Burger. She went for the Tempting Turkey. When they both had their food, they headed upstairs and claimed a table. She unwrapped her sandwich and held it out to him. "Tempted?" she asked, grinning big.

"Hell yes!" he laughed.

"Are you a vegetarian?"

"Sort of..."

Their conversation veered toward goofier stuff after he asked her if she'd ever been to Experience Music Project. She knew Geena had. When Geena's family had come over for dinner at Linny and Leonard's, she'd seen a bunch of photos of Geena's family looking like rock stars in there. She'd never been.

"So did you?" he persisted.

"Heck yeah!"

"Ever try karaoke?"

She was beginning to feel better. She was free! Ayden thought she was college material. Eugene arrived faster than any other town.

After he got off the train, she felt loneliness descend. She was used to feeling lonely, but for a few hours, she'd forgotten that fact.

Night proved to be long—and slow. She was lucky to have the pair of seats to herself. She put the back of her seat down. She set up the leg rest. She did the same for the other seat. That way she could sleep in different positions across the square of cushions. She used her parka for a blanket. A real blanket would have been nice. She should have thought of that. A blanket and a pillow. She did her best to snooze, dozing more often than she slept. Before long, her ass, her shoulders, and her neck ached.

One time, she sat up and looked out at the night to discover they were moving through a mountainous world. Another time, she woke and observed snow on the ground, illuminated by streetlights in some town. When she stirred and stretched into the morning, she figured they were closing in on the Bay Area. The sky was blue. Rays of the sun comforted her. She hadn't felt the sun in months.

She left her parka in her seat and cleaned up in the nearest head. Then she made her way to the snack bar with her precious backpack slung over one shoulder. She ordered a breakfast sandwich and a coffee, handing the café guy eight ones. One read *With Love from Jenny*. Oops! She headed back upstairs and sat in one of the seats facing the windows. The sandwich had that microwave feel. The coffee wasn't bad. Besides, she was going somewhere, and she had a view.

The train moved along at a rhythmic clip. Duh-duh. Duh-duh. Duh-duh.

They weren't expected in Los Angeles until 9 pm. Maybe she really should check out Santa Monica College, she thought idly. Though where would she live? She was achy from being on board for more than twenty-four hours. She kept thinking about the dark. When it came time for her to change trains in L.A., it would be dark outside Union Station. She probably wouldn't get to San Diego until after one in the morning. Leah didn't know she was coming.

She hadn't thought about the late arrival time when she'd bought her ticket. She'd just been pleased to note how the departure time worked well with her plan to get off the island before Linny and Leonard could figure out she was gone. She wondered if they'd bother to trace her. The ticket was in her name—the final destination, clear. Getting off somewhere else made sense! But where?

As the hours dragged past the Bay Area, the view began to wear thin. She remembered how Ayden had teased her about having a sore butt—she should have headed his warning. She was bored, and the café lunch menu was hardly something to look forward to, though she finally meandered downstairs to order a burger.

When the announcer called out the next stop—*San Luis Obispo*—she felt a sharp whim. She was still sitting in the Café Car, so she tossed her garbage and headed to her seat. She pulled on her coat, put on her backpack. She grabbed the little card that read SAN. She padded to the stairs that led to the exit thinking it was still light out.

SLO

Sadie stood by the tracks and gazed at the San Luis Obispo train station. Only two other passengers had gotten off here. In the waiting room she tossed the SAN card in the trash, then drew strength from the straps of her backpack, clutching more firmly. Now what?

Information.

She asked the man sitting there about the closest cheap hotel. The man told her it was a mile away. He drew a line on a map and handed it over. She felt a spark of gladness as she headed out the door. She could walk a mile, which she proceeded to do through this town that seemed a bit wealthy, but also regular.

The hotel was a regular chain.

"Could I see a credit card?" the receptionist asked. The woman reminded her of a Latina version of Bev, diamond wedding ring and all. She was probably a Latina, younger than Bev. She had a healthy head of dark brown hair hanging somewhat wildly about her shoulders.

"I've only got cash," Sadie said, her tone laced with worry.

"That will be $91 then."

As she pulled out her wallet, she realized the single dollar bills would make her look suspicious. She still had two of Linny's twenties. She handed those over first. "Sorry," she said, looking the woman in the eye. "I meant to get to the bank. To cash in my tips."

The receptionist peered at her.

"I work in a diner." She found herself gesturing with one hand. "I get tips."

"Money's money."

Sadie counted out another fifty-one dollars. Then she filled out a form, first thinking she should enter a phony name, but she changed her mind. If she wanted to find work, her name needed to match her ID and social. She would need to get to the bank tomorrow.

"Is there a Wells Fargo around here?" Maybe they could issue a debit card on the spot. She was dying to take Leonard's name off her account.

"About a mile away."

When she'd made the split-second decision to get off the train in San Luis Obispo, she worried her bank wouldn't be in this city. Now everything was on track. The receptionist was looking at her funny, so she pulled out the map she'd gotten from the guy in the train station. "Can you show me where it is?"

"Tomorrow is Sunday."

"I know," she replied nonchalantly, although she'd forgotten. Impatience flared. Now she'd have to wait till Monday to get her business done.

The room cost more than she wanted to spend, but it became a place to take a shower, watch some TV, get a good night's sleep, but mainly—stop worrying for a spell. Though it was time to get tough on herself. No more fancy drinks at Starbucks. She'd need to do everything on the cheap.

In the morning, she took advantage of the complimentary breakfast. She enjoyed dawdling through the last hour in her room. When she dropped off her keycard, she decided to pick the receptionist's brain.

"Hey, I'm trying to settle in here. I'm not sure where I'm going to live just yet."

The receptionist raised one eyebrow, half a smile.

"Do you know where I can find a cheaper hotel?"

"This is one of the cheapest," the woman answered glibly. "I think the Travelodge is about ten dollars less, maybe? It's a few miles away."

Sadie leaned into the counter, thinking hard. Ten dollars wasn't worth the stress of moving. It felt like a pretty careless thing to do, but she paid for another night.

"You want the same room?"

When she nodded, the receptionist did something to the keycard, before handing it back. "Enjoy your stay." The receptionist said this like she meant it.

Sadie returned to her room, which had not yet been made up. She counted her remaining cash. She had enough for a third night. The bank had to come through! Maybe they'd hassle her. Would they? So far from the island.

The next morning, she paid for another night before making her way to the bank, fretting the entire way. One of her fears immediately came true. They couldn't issue a debit card until she had an address in California. But she could withdraw some money with her ID. And they were willing to take Leonard's name off. That was the best news.

She strolled back through the glass doors with $407 dollars stowed in her backpack. She would stash it in her money belt later. Though it hurt big time to withdraw this much of her hard-earned savings, she needed a place to stay until she could find work and cheaper lodging. She needed to figure this out! Things could spin out of control so fast—that was what she was thinking as she walked through the commercial district to the hotel.

Up until this point, she'd had her plan to execute. Gather your things. Get out of their house. Get on the boat. Get on the train. Arrive. It had taken her full attention to work through each detail and make sure she was doing everything without fucking up. Each hurdle was a box to check. Each checked box made her feel a little more content, if not proud.

Now what?

Now the hard part was letting her know she could fail like her aunt said she would. Because Leah no longer figured into things. She had to admit she'd wanted Leah to put her up. But now there was nobody. She had no plan.

At the hotel she asked the receptionist if they had a computer with internet access. The receptionist nodded and pointed at a door partway down the hall.

She used her keycard to enter. The computer was on. Google was on the computer. She went to Craigslist and brought up San Luis Obispo. She clicked on **Food, Beverage & Hospitality**. One ad said she needed to clear a fingerprint check. She dismissed it, wondering if they had her fingerprints now that she'd stolen money from the restaurant (and that bitch!). There was a housekeeping gig for ten dollars an hour. But she didn't have that experience—just waitress work. She did find a part-time waitressing job that offered minimum wage plus tips. *Perfect!* She wrote down the address. The receptionist said it wasn't far.

"Sorry. We just filled that one," an older white man answered, after she inquired about the position. "If you'd like to complete an application, I can keep you on file."

She started to say "Yes," but then she realized she had no address—no phone.

She hiked back to the hotel.

"Is there anything I can help you with?" The receptionist's expression came with a bite.

"I never got your name," Sadie mumbled.

"Constanza."

"Constanza, I gotta find something long term. I mean, a place to stay," she blurted out, feeling a sense of recklessness surging. "And I gotta find work." She didn't know why she thought this woman could help—maybe because of how she reminded her of Bev. "I was hoping to get the job in that diner…" She waved her hand at the front door. "A few blocks from here, but they already found somebody."

Constanza looked her over. "So you're a waitress?"

"I was. I mean, in Washington. But I'm trying…"

"How old are you?"

"Eighteen."

"Let me see your ID."

Sadie handed it over and Constanza studied it closely. She said, "I do know of something that just opened up in Morro Bay. They were hoping for someone twenty-one or older, but they might consider you if you've got the right experience."

"Where's Morro Bay?"

"About thirteen miles from here. My eldest brother has a hotel there—and a restaurant. They need a waitress, ASAP. A good one! They might even offer a reduced rate on a room."

"That would be perfect!" She didn't dare to hope.

"During the off season, that is."

"What?"

"The reduced rate on the room is for the off-season. It would be minimum wage, but…" Constanza eyed her astutely, "You'd get your share of tips."

"Where do I sign?" she asked, trying to be fun.

"They use E-Verify. You know what that is?"

"They check my record?"

"They make sure you can work here legally."

"I just showed you my ID."

"You might be an Anglo, but my brother runs it on everyone. He was just burned by someone who gave him a phony ID. If you really want to know, one of his waiters ran off two days ago. Before he ditched Felipe, he cleaned out the till."

Constanza's eyes moved over her face as if she were trying to gauge how trustworthy she was. Sadie felt her gut flip. But she was already pleading on the inside for this to work, so her problems wouldn't go on and on, so she could end up somewhere and start a new life. But she was worried. She'd stolen more than two-hundred dollars from the person who would have given her a great recommendation. She'd stolen this money from the only person who really cared about her.

More than once, Bev had promised to give her raves when it came time for her to go after another job. Now she couldn't list her former boss as a reference. She'd blown her grades, her chance to go to college, and the best reference ever! Because Bev surely knew she'd stolen the dollars off the wall—Bev had a sixth sense about stuff like that. Had Bev turned her in? Would E-Verify even know? It was only two-hundred dollars. But she'd taken it from Bev!

"You OK?" Constanza asked.

"Just thinking this through."

Constanza told her where the bus stop was and wrote an address on a slip of paper, along with some more directions. "I'll call my brother to let him know you'll be applying."

It took a while for the bus to show up. The ride over was slow—so many stops! But she felt happy to let the bus carry her past the grassy green hills. She felt nervous about this interview with Felipe. *I'm a good waitress!* Bev even said so. But how was he going to know that?

When the bus turned into Morro Bay, she noticed three very tall smokestacks not far from the harbor. They were attached to some sort of power plant that seemed to be dead—there was no activity going on—maybe the place had closed. The smokestacks were too bad, she thought, because the second thing she spotted was this huge rock in the bay that appeared to be home to a whole lot of birds. Other than the smokestacks, the place came off stunning. It was cute and touristy and marine-like—like the island—but it didn't seem as wealthy as San Luis Obispo.

It wasn't a long walk to Felipe's establishment. Along the way, she looked over the cheerful businesses, the restaurants—an ice cream place. It was off-season, but there were plenty of people milling about.

At the restaurant Felipe greeted her warmly. "Constanza says you have experience," he smiled.

She discussed her two years in the diner, how she'd done about everything. In a pinch, Bev had allowed her to work the register.

"That's impressive for someone your age," he said, handing her an application, which she started to fill out. Then she said, "Um, Felipe. I don't have an address yet."

"What about your last address?"

"I'm between things, you know?"

He looked at her cockeyed.

"Constanza said I might be able to rent a room from you."

"Do you have an ID?"

She showed him her Washington driver's license.

"You live on an island?"

"I did," she said, as if it had been the most wonderful place ever. "I'm used to tourists."

"Fill out as much as you can. I'm also going to have you complete this I-9 form. That's for E-Verify. You can use your last address on that one."

She hated this! Would Felipe's computer just barf up everything wrong with her life and ultimately deem her a loser? *Just like your mother.*

Sadie did her best with both forms, before handing them over. She'd left a few gaps on the job application, because she didn't want Felipe to call Bev.

Felipe looked over her application and frowned. "I thought you had experience."

"I do. Really. Try me. You'll see."

He looked her in the eye. "Sadie... Did something go wrong?"

In a flash, she decided some honesty was better than one big lie. "I had to leave in a hurry. I didn't tell them I was going. I did work in a diner. Two years. It's a small town, so..."

"You didn't answer my question."

"I just turned eighteen. That means I could leave Linny and... Uh, my aunt and uncle, legally. They're my guardians, and they never…"

He stared her down, but she held her ground.

He sighed. "Tell you what. If E-Verify signs off on you, I'll give you a try. We really need someone reliable. Now! I've gone through several people in the past few months. I've had bad luck for some reason." Shaking his head, he continued, "It will be minimum wage. But you will be on probation. You hear me? Any messes, and you are so gone!"

"Could I rent a room then?" Felipe was a handsome man with light brown skin, dark brown eyes, and dark brown close-cropped brown hair with streaks of gray. She could tell from his quick smile he liked her spunk. "I can pay rent right away."

"Well…"

"I mean, Constanza said I might be able to live here at a reduced rate."

"If we hire you, you can stay in the back room for $500 a month. It's nothing special—comes with a bed, dresser, a shared half-bathroom. No shower."

She wrinkled her nose.

"You won't find anything cheaper."

"What about a TV?"

"If we hire you, we'll get you a TV. Besides, you'd have free Wi-Fi."

"Microwave?"

He shook his finger at her. "I'll see what I can do."

"When do I start?"

"Not till I hear back from E-Verify" He looked her up and down. "I probably shouldn't even bother." He sighed. "But I'm trying to be fair to the others."

She wasn't sure what he was getting at, but she smiled and nodded. She was bummed. The wait would mean more nights in the hotel, which would probably finish off the money she was carrying, if not more of her precious stash.

She bid Felipe farewell and walked around Morro Bay for a few hours. Yes! She liked this town that catered to visitors with fun-looking businesses. Morro Bay looked like a good place to set down her pack. She got on the bus to San Luis Obispo feeling a whirl of hopes moving through her, prompting her to make this work.

"How did it go?" Constanza asked.

"Good," she answered, with more conviction than she felt.

She headed for her room and crashed on the bed she was beginning to call her own. She'd told herself, no more drinks at Starbucks! No more meals out. But as the hours dragged into the next afternoon, she found herself losing control. She spent money in a way she never did on the island. Starbucks. Ice cream. Another drink at Starbucks. This was not smart, but she didn't know anyone. She did spot lots of people about her age hanging around San Luis Obispo, which made her feel shy. Probably Cal Poly students. Not her type.

The wait went on—there wasn't a lot to do. The next morning, she held up her cup of coffee and toasted the TV. The only thing on her schedule was to wash out her dirty clothes in the sink the way they did on Rick Steves.

Maybe she should check in with Bev. Confess. Pay Bev back, now that the debit card mess was solved. Well, almost. Leonard was off her account, but she still didn't have plastic. These thoughts shoved an uncomfortable sensation into her limbs, her gut. Bev was sure to be angry at her. Confessing would make her a thief. Being a thief meant Linny was right about her and her mother.

On Thursday evening, she bought a small take-out pizza and hauled it to her room. She was just getting settled when the telephone rang. It was Constanza. "Felipe says you're good to go."

OMG!

Morro Bay

During her first few weeks in the restaurant, Felipe watched her real close. Then he kept an eye out. She was fitting in—somewhat—and everyone was real nice. But it was clear she was an outsider. While plenty of Anglos ate at the restaurant, she was one of two working there. Felipe, his wife Isabel, and their other workers—several of whom were relatives—had stuff going on she wasn't privy to. This was true of their daily chats and the humor between them. In Bev's restaurant, things had been different. Bev had taken an interest in her life—Bev had become her friend. But these people had their own world.

Her room wasn't a real bedroom, though it was freshly painted, and the bed was comfy. It didn't have a closet. It did have a window. The bathroom was down the hall. She shared it with other workers, most of whom stayed somewhere else at night. Felipe and Isabel lived in a space attached to the hotel/restaurant—so they were around. Their five grown children were out of the house, though three lived in neighboring towns.

A housekeeper washed her sheets and towels once a week with the rest of the hotel laundry. Sadie washed her clothes in a nearby laundromat. Felipe did come through on the TV and microwave. He added a tiny fridge that doubled as a counter. She completed her kitchen after she discovered a thrift shop where she bought a plug-in kettle, a hot plate, a few pots, a set of mismatched dishes and utensils. Around town, she picked up miscellaneous items, like a pour over for coffee. One day, Felipe noticed a used Melitta filter in her trash and said, "I meant to give you a Mr. Coffee."

"That's OK, Felipe. I like how the coffee tastes this way."

"Trendy," he smiled, shaking head.

"Cool."

He pointed at her.

Her hunt continued. She spotted a freestanding coat rack through a thrift shop window. She found a set of shelves. Her Northwest apparel was out of place, so she looked for some sunnier clothes. She even managed to track down a used laptop so she could take advantage of the Wi-Fi .

The biggest pain was the bathroom down the hall. If she needed water for cooking or coffee, she was forced to use the sink in the bathroom. She used the same sink to rinse out her dishes. This sink was the source of hot water for her sponge baths and for shampooing her hair.

One of the other workers started complaining about how messy she was. She knew this because Isabel pulled her aside and led her to the tiny bathroom. The older woman pointed at two pieces of boiled macaroni glued to the bottom of the sink.

"Other people use this sink, Sadie. You need to keep it clean."

It was just two pieces of pasta—that's what she wanted to say. But she nodded and squeaked, "Oh. Sorry."

She'd begun to relax into the new situation, but Isabel's rebuke brought on a wave of tension that lasted for several days. She became hyperconscious over food in the sink. She didn't want to give them a reason to let her go. But then she went and blew it again! She left several strands of her blonde hair in the drain when she washed up.

"Sadie, I know it's hard. But you need to keep the sink clean," Isabel insisted.

She apologized once more, thinking the sponge baths were getting old. She'd had her own bathroom on the island. She could take a frickin' bath in there—or a shower. Her upstairs bedroom had been big with lots of light and a view of the forest that edged their yard. She'd had this huge closet, which she could sure use right now. She was finding it a challenge to organize her stuff.

Her inner whining was followed by a series of faded images focused on the seven-year-old who'd moved in with Linny and Leonard. Before that, she and her mother had lived in a shabby apartment in Renton. It was hard for her to dredge up her time with Cecilia—memories of neglect wouldn't cooperate with her need to see her mother as a beautiful person.

She had to admit she was feeling homesick—for Bev and other people she used to work with. She missed friends from school. One night, she looked herself up online to see if her absence from the island had been noticed. She Googled: *Sadie Taube Bainbridge Island.*

No missing persons announcement. No one was searching for her. She didn't want this thought to slice through her body, but "No one cares!" sank in before she had the chance to shove it back at the island. *No one cares!* She didn't like Linny. She thought her uncle was weak. Still, it hurt! Leonard used to protect Sadie from his wife. *In a way.* She didn't want it to hurt like this.

But when she checked her email account, she felt even worse, because someone was wondering where she was. There was a message from Bev: "Where are you?" And one from Leonard: "Where did you go?" These questions were in the subject line. She didn't bother to open them. Instead, she deleted her email account. She deleted her other accounts, like Instagram. She wouldn't be keeping up with her old life.

The money made her happy, though. Her bank was in Morro Bay. She didn't have to take the bus to San Luis Obispo to make deposits. *Finally!*

On the day when she gave the bank her new address so she could order a replacement debit card, the teller said, "Looks like a new deposit just came in."

"What?"

"From See Birds Diner. Bainbridge Island, Washington."

"How much?"

"$421."

Bev shouldn't have, she thought. Bev should have docked her pay. Maybe she should send Bev a check for $200 now that she'd added a checking account to the debit card. That would be the right thing to do. Then she and Bev could still be friends. Like maybe she could call Bev up and ask her about restaurant stuff, because she didn't have anyone to lean on. But then everyone would know where she was. Linny might decide to show up on Felipe's doorstep and insist Sadie stop embarrassing them. "She needs to give back." That was how Linny liked to put it. *After all we've done for you!*

She could send cash to Bev and not include a return address... But there would still be a postmark.

Felipe stopped watching her work so carefully—her habits around the place, which she kept intentionally dull. Anything cool would have to go on outside of here! Felipe said she was pretty good at everything. She made sure she kept it that way. When summer crept up, he let her keep the room. He didn't even jack the rent. This stirred some trouble with Isabel. She overheard a conversation between them when she was sitting on the toilet in the half-bathroom.

"We could get more for that room, Felipe."

"She's a duckling."

As Sadie wiped her rear, she imagined Isabel shaking her head. But Felipe got his way. She stayed. It wasn't long before another winter was upon her.

Felipe became concerned about her predicament with Linny and Leonard, which she'd shared in bits and pieces when prompted, though not the whole story—not the heroin part. He thought she needed to get a California Driver's license. "You're earning money in California now," he said, handing her a little booklet that outlined the rules of the road in her new state. "You need a California ID for all sorts of things."

One afternoon, Felipe strolled past her and declared, "You need to meet someone."

"When do I have the time?"

He did have her working a lot, which was good, because she was pulling in tips. And though she was paying rent for the first time in her life, her savings was still growing, because now she could work full-time! She could work overtime.

"I've got nephews," Felipe noted.

She found this line of talk awkward. The new situation was working—and it was a relief. But she didn't have the energy to do anything but hold it together.

During her free time, she took walks on the beach, or she read in her room, or she lay on her bed to stare at the ceiling, breathing into her blank mind. She watched TV when she was really bored. Or she surfed the net. She didn't want to spend money on anything extra. Boyfriends cost extra—they didn't always pay for everything. She kept saving as much as she could.

One winter day, she decided to head to the DMV. She filled out some paperwork and took another written test. *She passed!* When her new driver's license arrived in the mail, she felt a bite in her gut that held firm a while. Bev had loved the Washington one, but she was a Californian now.

Gonzalo

One month after her nineteenth birthday, Sadie was trying to get two orders straight. She untangled the snafu and proceeded to cart the right meals to the right tables, before noticing the sunset angling into the restaurant like transparencies, those sheets of plastic her biology teacher had used to illustrate things. The gleaming light made her feel a tad bit giddy, and as she continued to serve people, she let this feeling show.

"I really love the enchiladas here," a white woman said.

"I'll tell Felipe." She smiled back.

She stuck this woman's order into a clip attached to a line of other orders, fluttering dull green rectangles, and turned in time to spot Felipe as he led a family to a table with a partial view of the bay. As the group of five ambled in close contact with each other, they seemed to signify how well they were doing as a unit. She wished she had a family like that. Then she spotted the best pairing of shiny dark hair and dark brown eyes she'd ever seen. This remarkable face belonged to a man somewhat older than her, maybe 5 or 7 years. He was accompanied by a woman who appeared to be his wife, as well as a much older couple (the parents?), and a teenage girl. The girl wore jeans that sparkled, while her toes displayed an admirable red pedicure atop cork platform sandals.

Her gaze returned to the man. He wasn't flashy, though he was nicely dressed in button-down mauve shirt and black slacks, black leather shoes. He wore a wedding ring. These impressions shot around her brain as she lifted a tray of soft drinks and carried it to the other side of the room.

As the evening progressed, she tried not to study the guy. Because of the ring. She didn't want her boss to know how she was feeling about this gorgeous human being. Felipe noticed everything. Of course, there were a lot of good-looking men in Morro Bay, but this one—he was pretty good looking—but it wasn't that. She wasn't sure what it was she was responding to. No, she didn't want Felipe or Isabel tuning in to her attraction. She didn't want the guy to notice. She had no idea what his name was.

Fortunately, Constanza entered the restaurant with her youngest daughters, Luna and Luciana, twins who were about six. The trio often ate at the restaurant without Constanza's husband, Mateo. Mateo usually worked late into the evening.

Sadie greeted the new arrivals and grabbed three menus from a holder on the wall. When she smiled big at this woman who'd helped her gain a foothold, Constanza nodded. Sadie grinned at her daughters. They giggled—sweet girls—both missing their upper front teeth.

"Someone's been visited by the tooth fairy," Sadie pointed out, looking closely at their mouths.

This earned her two even bigger grins, truly revealing the gaps where teeth had been.

"You want the usual table, Constanza?" But she was already leading them to the one she knew they favored.

Over the next hour, she gave the girls heaps of attention. She wondered out loud if their front teeth might never grow back, making them respond in mock horror.

"How will you eat any chips?" she asked, before setting down a basket of fresh ones to the tune of young laughter in stereo.

Luna eyed her astutely before grabbing a good-sized handful of chips and stuffing them into her mouth. She chewed and grinned and chewed and grinned. Constanza shook her head, though a trace of a smile hovered. That's when Sadie placed her hands on her hips to stare this child down. Luna was so completely adorable, with crumbs all over the front of her pink T-shirt. She was just thinking the words super cute when Luciana decided she needed a handful of chips. The twins began chewing in unison.

"Girls, close your mouths when you eat," Constanza said.

Later, Sadie noticed more salsa was called for on Constanza's table, and she brought it by. She shot a glance at Felipe, who was still chatting with the older couple attached to the dreamboat man and his wife—the teenage girl. *Was this magnificent man one of Felipe's nephews?* That would mean he was also Constanza's nephew.

"Constanza," she asked offhandedly. "Are those friends of Felipe?"

"Oh yes! Longtime friends."

Not their nephew. She filed this information away for further contemplation.

Summer passed, a whirl of taffy, trinkets, and happy tourists. She was feeling better, though there were things she missed about the island: the deep mossy forests, snow-capped Olympics, ferry rides. She missed Bev like crazy. She wanted to pay her back, but she felt weird about admitting what she'd done. She wasn't certain Bev knew she'd taken the money. She'd selected her bills carefully, and when she'd left that night, the diner had looked the same. That was what she told herself. And anyway, Bev wasn't using the money on the wall. The money was there for fun. It sure would be awkward to confess, only to discover Bev had no clue.

Relationships

On her day off, Sadie found herself sitting in a locally owned coffee house. She leaned back and sipped from a cup of French roast, a treat she allowed herself on occasion, so she could take in the ambience of Morro Bay. She liked the feel of the place, where locals congregated and chatted—or they read stuff—some were doing homework. As she relaxed, her gaze drifted to a pile of course schedules for the community college—they were stacked near the "Community Board." *Hmm.* She pushed her chair back and got up to grab a copy. As she paged through it, she was surprised to notice the school wasn't too expensive. *Maybe...* Maybe I could pass the GED and work on something like nursing. She'd heard there were lots of nursing jobs. She'd heard they paid pretty well. But then Linny and Leonard's dinner table flashed into her brain. "Your grades are disappointing, honey," Leonard had said. "You'll never make it in college," Linny sneered.

She shook her head at the whole idea of a GED. *I need to earn more money.* Her bank account was the one thing she was accomplishing in this world. Occasional offers for dates came her way, but she usually declined, devising strategies for avoiding those who might be interested. Though she finally went out with a guy named Sterling. He had light brown hair, shoulder length—blue eyes—a tan. He wore a silver hoop in one ear. "See," he pointed. "Sterling."

They dated for about five months, during which time, she could feel Felipe and Isabel collectively holding their breath. She wanted the relationship to be right, so she could be normal, maybe live with a guy instead of a Hispanic restaurant crew. Her new boyfriend inhabited a one-bedroom apartment. It was decorated with original paintings and framed black and white photographs. His furniture was what she'd call arty, with unusual colors and lines, while the rug covering a good portion of the hardwood floor displayed a burst of geometrical designs.

When Sterling said the rug was from Bali, she found herself yearning for her own place. She was drawn to his aesthetic. Yet when they slept together during the day (she never spent the night on account of Felipe and Isabel—too weird), she didn't feel anything special, though it was nice to hold him on a Sunday afternoon. She didn't love Sterling, but she did like the fact that he was cool.

One day Sterling told her he'd met someone else. He told her he hadn't acted on his attraction, but he did want to explore things. *What should we do?* She'd left in a huff—carrying some soreness—but it was over.

"What happened to the boyfriend?" Felipe asked one morning.

"Don't ask!"

"Sadie..." He was shaking his head. "What are we going to do with you?"

"I'm working on it," she answered firmly. But her usual routine held, including the overtime she'd begun putting in when one of the waiters submitted his resignation. Felipe had his eye out for a new employee.

A few months after she turned 20, she stood before the "Community Board" in the coffee house. This time she spotted an advertisement for a yoga class. She stared at it a long while, before memorizing the address so she could plug it into the calendar on her laptop. She needed something to do.

The class was taught by a wiry white yogini named Alexis. "Sadie, see if you can put more weight into the balls of your feet. That's it. Now look for ways to deepen the stretch." Sadie pulled her hips back, while also trying to lengthen her torso.

"Nice, Gillian!" Alexis cheered. Gillian was a round redhead with a bushy ponytail and green eyes that looked warm whenever Sadie managed to meet them.

There were about thirteen other folks in the class of various ages, races, and sizes. The room felt safe, particularly when "namaste" sounded out and people began rolling up their mats. She liked the open friendliness these yogis and yoginis conveyed.

Some months later, she found herself in a de facto 20-something club with Alexis and Gillian. Their friendship blossomed after Alexis invited Sadie and Gillian to her cottage for tea. "When's your day off, Sadie?" At twenty-eight, Alexis was the oldest of this newly formed trio.

While she wasn't sure about tea or new-agey shit, she decided to sync her calendar with theirs. She was surprised to enjoy a fine afternoon talking and laughing with these two women who were working on their lives in Morro Bay. Making money was the toughest part for all three. They discovered this during one passionate discussion. They loved this town—they all said it—but keeping it together was a challenge—that's what they all agreed.

Gillian lived at home, but she wanted to get a place ASAP. Alexis—lucky her—had scored over the clapboard cottage with its shiny hardwood floor, large windows, and good light. The living room came off like a yoga studio with little clutter and a few pieces of well-chosen furniture—some impressionist prints on the walls. As the three of them yakked, Sadie could hear wind chimes clanging. She openly admired the yogini's ability to put a place together, feeling compelled to ask about how she'd gotten it, but then a shy streak held her back.

Her new friends continued to deliver interesting conversations and fun times. Her stash was nice and healthy. She was feeling as good as she'd ever felt.

"Maybe it's time for you to find a bigger place, Duckling," Felipe suggested one afternoon. When she winced back at him, he held up his hands. "A beautiful young woman like you deserves better."

"I'm not ready," she replied shortly.

"Felipe, let Sadie decide," Isabel cut in. "She's just finding a foothold."

Sadie grinned at Isabel with all the gratitude she could muster. Isabel had come to understand.

"Say no more," he said.

When she was almost twenty-one, she was surprised when three celebrations came her way. A week before her birthday, she received a gift certificate for a local boutique from Felipe and Isabel. They made her sit down with them (and Constanza and the twins) for dinner "on the house." Conversation that night was lively, though one point in the evening found Felipe shaking his head. "Gonzalo and Teresa are getting divorced," he said. "The family is heartbroken."

She fought the reaction wanting to break out like mad. *OMG*. She now knew Gonzalo was the beautiful man who sometimes came into the restaurant with his family. While she'd never spoken to him directly—she'd found ways to skirt this—she learned his name one evening when she overheard Felipe beckoning him. "Gonzalo, do you have a moment?" Gonzalo. She'd been so happy after that because she could hold his name inside. He was the one aspect of life in Morro Bay she never mentioned to Alexis and Gillian.

But she thought about him. All. The. Time.

After she thanked Felipe and his family for the fine evening, Felipe told her she absolutely could not work on her twenty-first birthday. "Get out there!"

She informed Alexis about the unexpected night off, only to find herself with a second invitation. Alexis offered to have her and Gillian over in honor of her birthday, an event replete with balloons, presents, dinner, and a carrot cake. Alexis had soothing music on, the windows wide open. Gusts of wind blew silky air through the living room, the chimes into a melody. Gillian contributed a bottle of wine, though Alexis remained on the wagon. "I've sworn it off," she insisted. "But Sadie, you're twenty-one! You have to celebrate." Alexis ended up sipping from a non-alcoholic concoction as Gillian and Sadie passed the bottle of Cabernet back and forth.

Later that night, she looked around her cluttered room that was not a real bedroom but was now home. She felt safe with Felipe and Isabel. She thought about Bev, wondering if her former boss had remembered her birthday. She wondered about her aunt and uncle, how they'd never bothered to look for her. She doubted they'd stopped to consider this milestone in her life. Twenty-damn-one! Felipe was already teaching her how to handle the bar.

A week later, Gillian dragged her to a bona fide watering hole, a realm that up until then had been a murky mystery, one Sadie passed sometimes as it released puffs of fermentation if the door happened to swing open. Gillian was twenty-three—she'd been enjoying Morro Bay's nightlife for a while. This particular haunt was Gillian's favorite, dark and boozy—noisy. They claimed one corner and ordered drinks, chatting about where Gillian might live so she didn't have to feel like a teenager.

"So Sadie, I'm like... Mom!" Gillian gripped her margarita. "'I really need to find my own place.' And she's like... Gillian, when I was getting started, it was easy to afford a decent apartment.' And Mom's just shaking her head when Dad comes in and says, 'Mom's place was wonderful!' And then they start kissing, way too long. And I'm like sighing out loud. 'Like I can't even afford to rent a room in this town!' And they're like turning to look at me. 'Honey, you know we'll leave you the house.'"

"Yeah right, a hundred years from now," Sadie commiserated.

They downed way too many margaritas, moving into an even deeper conversation. A blast! After they left the bar, they decided to make this a weekly date. So Sadie had yoga and margaritas. Sadie had a lot of work to do for Felipe. That was her life.

College

She needed a plan.

After making herself a cup of coffee early one morning, she settled against her pillows and brought up the community college on her laptop so she could look over the admissions process. The idea of getting a GED continued to prick her. As she scanned the page, she noticed a passage she didn't expect to find: "Persons over the age of eighteen without a high school diploma can enroll if, in the judgment of the President, they are capable of benefiting from the instruction offered."

Was she capable of benefiting? Her high school GPA sucked! What was she supposed to do, knock on the president's door and plead for a chance?

As she waited tables that night, she thought about how much college might cost—this was if the president allowed her to enroll. Would a degree really help her make more money? Why would they bother with someone like her, with her 2.7 GPA and no high school diploma? Why would they bother with a thief? She'd have to do some fast-talking to get a toe in. That's what she figured.

She remembered how, when she first arrived, she'd convinced Felipe she was right for the job. That hadn't been easy, but it had worked. Felipe liked her now. Even Isabel liked her. No, she wasn't college material! Linny had been convinced she'd resort to drugs. Well, Linny had been wrong! She was clean, and proud of it. But a familiar icky-off feeling overtook her. Linny had not been wrong about the stealing. She'd skipped the drugs and just started stealing. That was what Felipe and Isabel didn't know about her. Though she hadn't stolen a thing since her last night on the island. And now that she'd adopted Morro Bay, she needed to get her head straight. She just didn't know how.

One evening, she and Gillian were sipping margaritas in the watering hole when she blurted out what she'd never said to anyone.

"My mother died of a heroin overdose."

As she watched Gillian's face fall, she marveled at herself for this moment of honesty. She stared at Gillian hard, expecting a blast of judgment. But Gillian said, "I'm so sorry." And Gillian meant it!

So she continued with her story, feeling relief seeping into her. At some point, she talked about how she'd started a savings account in high school. That was why she'd found the courage to leave the island, which had never been a home.

"You're such a role model, Sadie!" Gillian marveled. And she felt a spark of surprise. She didn't deserve that one, she reasoned.

"I just want a better life than what my mother had." Come to think of it, she wanted to live better than Linny and Leonard. Those two weren't happy! This was the first time she'd considered such a thought.

The intimacy of the evening moved into Gillian's story.

The yogini confessed she sometimes took pain meds to feel OK. At first, they felt fine, no addiction. Nothing. But then they started making her dopesick. "I don't want to rely on Vicodin to get through life." That was why Gillian had taken up yoga. "It's hard, though," she confessed. "Sometimes, I don't have what it takes…"

"That's not true!" Sadie insisted, wanting to be helpful to her friend, because she was beginning to love this mischievous woman, irrespective of her impulsive choices. She was pretty sure Gillian was falling into heavier partying—Gillian sometimes relayed accounts of bad sex, if not rape. She decided not to comment on any of this—to listen. But she wasn't really a role model. She couldn't shake the disappointment Bev must harbor, the word thief. But that was there—on the island! All the disappointment reserved for Sadie Taube was floating above Bainbridge Island.

She felt settled in Morro Bay. This thought still surprised her. But all she was doing was saving money. Every small pleasure she might buy would run through some accounting program in her brain. "Can I really afford this?" She often said no, foregoing something that could have been good. Now that she had a few friends, she did spend a little more on herself, but not without hand-wringing. What she needed to do was make even more money, so she could live better—so she would feel fine about going out to dinner or taking a class. She'd been clinging to her bank account like it was some kind of life raft. She didn't know how to get out of that raft!

She remembered Ayden, that guy she'd met in the train station. He'd suggested she might be good at business. So maybe she could convince the college president she was capable of benefiting from business classes. *What could it hurt?* She jotted down the president's number. Though, what would she say when this president answered? "Hi, I didn't graduate from high school, but I'm capable of benefiting from business." She rehearsed her opening lines several times. It took her three days to work up the nerve to make the call. When she finally punched in the number, she was immediately thrown by the woman on the other end. "This is Charlene Burger, administrative assistant to Joy Lin, college president. How can I help you?"

"I uh, I need to speak to President Lin."

"What is the nature of your call?"

"That I'm capable of benefiting from business. Classes, I mean."

"I see. And you need to speak to the president about this?"

"Uh…" She knew they were lying! About people without diplomas. This lady didn't think she should be calling up the big ass president. She was about to click off the phone, but then she heard the tinny sound of "Hello, hello…" Coming through her cell phone.

What the fuck? She sighed on the inside. "Well… I uh, I never graduated from high school, and I don't have my GED."

The administrator responded right back. "Then let's get you in for an appointment."

What?

Major relief was what she experienced until she thought about what it would feel like to actually meet with President Lin. She hadn't dealt with a big ass woman in a while.

The next morning, she told Isabel what was up.

"That sounds like a fine plan, Sadie."

But she was really nervous when she was directed into the president's office, and Ms. Lin stood up to shake her hand. They were about the same height, she noticed. She looked at the woman closely, trying to scope her out. President Lin had small bones and no extra weight. She had long black hair. Like she was almost hip. Sadie digested the three framed degrees on the wall. One from U. C. Riverside. Two from UCSB. "Hello, President Lin." She'd rehearsed this opener and was glad when she remembered it right.

"Joy," the president replied. "You can call me Joy." President Joy's smile moved into her eyes.

That would be easier, she decided, before launching into her plan to become a business major. Sadie wasn't sure how she actually put everything to the president—Joy—she felt her words coming out in one whirling blur.

She talked about starting a business—or working for a bigger company—how she'd never graduated from high school—that was why she was working for Felipe right now.

"Can I ask how much high school education you did attain?"

"Almost all of it," she said, realizing this answer didn't sound so bad. She'd pretty much finished high school. She'd just never gotten the piece of paper. "I left right before my last quarter."

"Sounds like you might be a good fit."

"Really?" She'd been convinced they were going to badger her about no diploma. Then she remembered her grades. "But my grades aren't great."

"Do you remember your last GPA?"

"I think… Uh… 2.7." She tried not to wince.

President Joy nodded. "Let's give it a try."

She couldn't believe it! She was going to be a college student.

Joy went on to discuss the application process. She described the assessment tests Sadie would need to take.

"So I have to take a test before you know if I'm good enough?"

From the time she'd walked into the office, she'd had the feeling President Lin was being way too rosy. An assessment test. Yuck! This was how the college would spit her out.

But the president leaned forward onto her desk, and Sadie noticed how she had very few lines in her face. *How old was she?* "You'll definitely be allowed to start, Sadie. We just need to know where to place you."

She must have looked fearful because the president's gaze drilled into her own. "When we place students in courses they aren't ready for, they often get discouraged and quit. We don't want that to happen to you! We want you to be successful. That's why we offer lots of options for our students, especially with the math and English classes. I have no doubt there's a place for you here."

Did this Joy woman really mean that? She couldn't believe college would work out, though she felt dreamy as she meandered across the campus on her way back to the bus stop. She tried to imagine herself on these sidewalks for real.

A week later, she took all the required tests, feeling her shoulders scrunching into her ears. When she was finally admitted as a provisional student, Felipe shouted, "Hooray!" And Isabel said, "Congratulations, Sadie!"

Her scores weren't bad. She did pretty well on the math and could begin at college level, but she was placed in a pre-college writing course. She decided to start slow because she was attending part-time.

Felipe rearranged her work schedule to fit with her new college one. When she left for her first day of school, he smiled his oversized smile. Sadie blew him a kiss. She rode the bus to the campus, located between Morro Bay and San Luis Obispo. As she stepped into the fray—with people everywhere—she was certain they were staring. College people thought they were better than her. She wasn't a college student! But when she got to math, the instructor was friendly. The syllabus offered the lowdown. Maybe? In high school, she hadn't always done her work— she knew that.

The new routine kept her hopping. Yoga fell by the wayside. She rarely had time for margaritas with Gillian. Though once she finished her first semester, she started to relax and say "Hi" to people. Sometimes, they studied in groups. She went out on a couple of dates, though nothing took hold.

On the first day of her fourth semester, she opened the door to her new business class and spotted Gonzalo. *OMG!* He was sitting in the classroom with his back to her. They were in the same class! She stopped beneath the doorway feeling energy shooting through her body, making her want to move, run a race, dance a crazy dance. Gonzalo was sitting there! She checked out his left hand. No ring. She moved to the seat next to his.

When he smiled right at her, his brown eyes danced.

She smiled back.

"You work for Felipe."

"I do," she said, before she realized what that sounded like. Oh no!

Yet it was easy, talking to him, as she'd known it would be. Was he dating? But she asked, "Are you a business major?"

"I want to open a restaurant."

She was impressed he already had a plan. She didn't know what kind of business she wanted. That's what she said back to him. And then they were forced to pay attention to the instructor who was standing at the front of the room.

Two days later, Sadie ran into Gonzalo in the cafeteria. She'd already grabbed a coffee, which she held in one hand. "Have a seat," he said, grinning at her as he gestured at the chair across from him. She smiled and sat down as if they'd always done this. That was when she discovered how he liked to talk.

Over subsequent weeks, she learned Gonzalo had married Teresa right after high school ended. Things between them eventually went bad, and it about killed his parents to watch him go through a divorce. Fortunately, they never had kids. This was because Teresa insisted on attending the university before starting a family. Meanwhile, Gonzalo's father urged him to join the family contracting business, but Gonzalo knew it wasn't his thing. This had been hard on the old man, but he and Teresa needed to find their own way. Teresa ended up enrolling at Cal Poly, while he became a cook. He wanted to become a high-class chef—he had a few other odd jobs. When Teresa was well into her master's program, that was when they decided to get divorced. At the time, he was working for a posh restaurant in San Luis Obispo. Now he was thinking he could start his own restaurant—do things his own way. He planned to finish a Culinary Arts certificate, but he was also boning up on business.

They began doing their homework together, especially when finals were coming up. They were good at different things. Sadie had a knack with numbers. She was seriously considering becoming an accountant—her counselor was already encouraging her on this path. She could get her AS in Business Administration with an accounting specialization. "If you do well enough, you can transfer to Cal Poly. You could work on becoming a CPA."

This thought was too much for her. She needed to catch up—in English, especially. Fortunately, writing was Gonzalo's specialty. He was willing to help whenever she had a paper due. Gonzalo loved to read poetry.

As the weeks passed, he proved to be great at writing ads for the marketing class they were both taking. Sadie was jealous of his writing. She admired how funny he was in school and in the world. His lame romantic lines made her laugh inside. He liked to recite poetry with his wide-open eyes on hers.

"She walks in beauty, like the night..."

But she didn't encourage anything, though she did watch for signs of other women in his life. He was friendly with many women, but he didn't seem to be focusing on anyone. He still talked about Teresa, though. Teresa was the one who'd insisted on the divorce. It wasn't hard to guess this was a source of pain for him. Who wanted to be dropped cold?

Driving

During Sadie's fifth semester, Gonzalo asked her out. She was ready for this! He drove her up Highway One in his pickup, showed her some more towns. It was sunny and the waves curled turquoise.

"Do you drive, Sadie?"

She nodded. "I'm rusty, though. I can't afford a car."

They continued on past Hearst Castle but did not check it out. They did stop at Piedras Blancas elephant seal rookery, where they strolled along a walkway parallel to the sea. This afforded them a look at a pile of cumbersome bodies on the beach, the way the seals waddled to take a dip in the ocean, the way the alpha males got into standoffs. She could see their weird noses flapping. But mostly, the elephant seals looked content, all crowded together, more relaxed than yoginis.

"They're hilarious," she laughed.

He reached for her hand and maybe a mysterious feeling came over her, whatever it was that had first made her notice him. Maybe the mysterious feeling was a real thing that could happen to a real person. And maybe she felt it more acutely now that she had a chance with him. She held his hand in hers until they were back at the truck.

"You want to take the wheel?"

"You mean it?" Her eyes grew big.

He handed her the keys and they switched seats.

"I didn't get to drive much before I left the island."

She felt self-conscious as he watched her start the truck. She remembered how to put it in reverse, but she felt tense. She checked all the mirrors, before cranking her head back to make sure the coast was clear. She backed out feeling stiff, but he didn't comment on her slowpoke ways. She put the truck in drive. When she turned north onto Highway 1, she smiled. "I'm not used to windy roads," she said, trying to keep her speed even.

Gonzalo turned to look out the rear window. "Don't let them push you around," he urged. "Yes, yes!" he encouraged. "Go, go, Sadie!" She was leading a snake of cars, and this made her feel more nervous, because she wasn't sure about racing through the curves. She didn't want the car to flip. "Go, go, go!" Gonzalo shouted. She tried to drive a little faster, gripping the wheel. Gripping. On a straight stretch she wouldn't mind putting the pedal down.

He gave her directions to a parking lot with beach access. She parked the truck, feeling happy when she shut off the engine.

"You want to walk?"

They headed down the beach holding hands once more, the waves breaking over and over.

"You're sad," he said.

She liked his way of asking without asking, so she answered him. "My mom died of a heroin overdose." She never used to tell anyone this. Telling Gillian had shifted something inside of her. She no longer wanted to pretend it didn't happen.

"Where's your father?"

"No idea," she shrugged.

"C'mere," he said, leading her to a smooth place in the bluff. They sat and kissed there, for how long, she did not know. "How's that?" he finally asked.

"Nice."

On the way back, they stopped for fish and chips at a small café near Cambria. It reminded her of Bev's place, but she didn't bring this up to Gonzalo. She wouldn't think about her boss right now because she was living a perfect day.

He drove her home and they kissed some more after he put the truck in park. "If you want to keep practicing, let me know."

"Kissing?" She was thinking he was being pretty salty.

"Driving, silly."

On their fourth date, they made love in his tiny studio. After that, she kept an eye on their grades. "We need to stay on track," she said.

"We'll study," he agreed.

Gonzalo was in the habit of studying at his parents' house. One Sunday afternoon, he invited her to join him in their 1950s era home, which had a formal dining area. Just as she was wondering where his parents were, Gonzalo said, "Pop's probably in his man cave and Mama has a detached studio in the backyard. I'm pretty sure she has a sewing project underway."

When she nodded, he motioned toward the rectangular dining room table, perhaps made of cherry wood. It was surrounded by eight ladderback chairs. "We've got plenty of room to spread our stuff," he said.

She looked over at one wall painted ochre. It was covered with photos. Her interest prompted a smile on the part of Gonzalo. "I'll introduce you to those folks later," he said, making her wonder if he meant the photos or the actual people.

"Sure," she answered, unzipping her purple backpack. "How many brothers and sisters do you have?"

"Two sisters. My big sis—Carla—lives in Sacramento. She is married with two kids. She's been out of the house for years. Works in HR for Sac State." He waved at the graduation photo of a girl with long dark hair and sparkling brown eyes. "Carmen is the baby. She still lives here. But hey…" He paused and squeezed her shoulder. "We've got work to do."

They organized their papers across half the long table. They fired up their laptops. They had the same assignment to do for BUS 202.

"We both know what my business plan is going to be," he pointed out wryly. "What's your plan?"

She had to reach for this answer because she didn't have a plan. She didn't want to copy his, though her experience was in the restaurant business. She tried to come up with something different. Something cool. "I like what Rick Steves does."

He laughed out loud. "A travel company?"

"Like maybe for America. Like what Rick Steves is doing. Only for America." She remembered putting together her big train trip—how she'd taken advice from Rick's videos and books as she'd planned her journey. "The company would be about traveling in America. Through the backdoor."

"Hmmph!"

"So you finally brought Sadie."

They turned in unison to say hello to Gonzalo's mother, who had her hand out. Sadie shook it. "Great to meet you, Mrs. Vargas. I've seen you in Felipe's restaurant."

"You may call me Mia," his mother smiled. "His father is Dylan," she gestured behind her. Sadie hadn't noticed him standing there.

"Felipe sure has some good things to say about you." Dylan grinned as he shook her hand. Sadie smiled into a long pause as both of Gonzalo's parents looked her over.

"Well, we won't interrupt your homework," Mia cut in, "but I wanted to invite you both for dinner. Will you stay?"

Gonzalo turned to look at Sadie inquiringly.

"Sure," she said, feeling most pleased by the unexpected gush of sweetness. It was like they were the ones courting her.

Sometime later, they were all seated around the dinner table—and this included Gonzalo's younger sister Carmen.

"My baby's going to be the first in the family to earn a college degree," Dylan boasted, as Carmen passed Sadie a heavy dish. Sadie looked inside to spot chicken smothered in a dark brown sauce. Not knowing completely what it was, she stabbed a piece for her plate. She was about to hand the dish to Gonzalo, when he said, "You'll want to put more of that mole on your chicken."

"What?"

"Mama makes the best mole."

She decided not to ask what mole was, but she did take Gonzalo's advice. When she finally took a bite, she said, "Wow! I mean, mmm. What's in this sauce?"

"Chocolate," Gonzalo replied.

"Sweet!"

She and Gonzalo continued receiving positive reinforcement whenever they studied at the Vargas family home. As they hunched over their assignments, or studied for finals, Mia and Dylan were never far away, puttering, working on this project or that one. Something was always bubbling in the kitchen, which made the place smell homey and nice. Invariably, one would pop a head in to make sure they had everything. "How's it going?" They were proud of Gonzalo for attending college at his age, even as he pulled his weight for the family—helping with Carmen's tuition and books. They were definitely proud of that. Occasionally, Mia threw Teresa's name into the conversation. Like "Gonzalo and Teresa used to go to Catalina Island…" Whenever this happened, Gonzalo would give her a look and say, "Mama…"

Sadie wondered if they'd prefer a Latina for Gonzalo. She tried not to let that thought get to her, but she didn't fit in with the Vargas family. She was from another planet.

When she and Gonzalo were alone in his studio one evening, she finally pounced. "Why did you and Teresa divorce?"

He shrugged, and she could feel how she was trespassing, but she wanted to know.

"You parents really like her."

"Oh, don't mind them. They had their hearts set on that marriage when we were little kids."

"Your mother…"

"I think we married because they wanted us to get married. All four parents wanted it. They started bringing it up when we were about twelve." Her expression must have telegraphed discomfort because he reached for her hand. "Really, Sadie. Teresa is the daughter of Pop's business partner. My parents are already in love with you."

She doubted this was true because being with Gonzalo's parents made her feel tense. They acted friendly, but their home wasn't her place. This unhappy thought made her consider her place in Felipe's restaurant, her place in the yoga studio—her place at the college. These were her places. These were the places she'd found on her own.

"But what you had with Teresa sounded ideal," she asserted. "The two families behind you. Gonzalo, why didn't the marriage work?"

"It just didn't," he growled.

Slowly, she figured things out because Mia kept offering tidbits. "They went to the prom together," she revealed. "They both worked on the school newspaper."

While Sadie didn't think Mia was being intentionally mean over these travels down memory lane, her stories were beginning to grate.

"Teresa was a top student in high school," Mia noted one afternoon as the never-ending story of the young couple barreled forward. Sadie had begun taking painstaking inner notes on Teresa, which she reviewed at regular intervals.

Teresa had been a Fulbright Scholar—Teresa won other awards. Teresa was now in a doctoral program at UCSB, expecting to become a history professor. Teresa was mentoring Carmen, who was keeping it together at Cal Poly, because Teresa kept checking in with her, offering advice and support.

Sadie knew what had happened to this marriage! Teresa was a racehorse. She could fit in anywhere. Meanwhile, Gonzalo had worked full-time—more than full-time. He didn't start at the community college until after they were divorced. So maybe Gonzalo couldn't take the fact that his former wife was becoming a big ass professor!

Matrimony

Gonzalo shocked her with a marriage proposal. This was too fast—Sadie knew that—but she didn't care.

"Yes," she said, and deep romance ensued.

"Will you help me open the restaurant?"

"Double yes!"

She thought about Bev and Nate, trying to ignore the shot of pain that could still surface over what she'd lost. A restaurant was a fine business. She could do the books once she got her AS and her accounting certificate. She already knew how to do pretty much everything else, though she'd never created a menu or ordered supplies. She wished she could talk to Bev about that. They would need to hire some help. Gonzalo was the best cook. Mia had taught him everything. They had that part covered. Though they'd probably need more than one cook.

"Mama wants to help you plan the wedding."

"You told them?"

He smiled and gave her another kiss. "They're happy, Sadie."

Wow!

When she appeared for her next shift, Felipe strolled past wearing a big grin. "Congratulations, Duckling!"

"Does everyone in this town know about the wedding?" She placed her hands on her hips, but she was laughing. She was feeling good.

A week later, she sat down with Mia to think about the ceremony and the reception. Mia asked what their plans were once they tied the knot. She tried to outline their future for her mother-in-law to-be. She said it would be a while before she and Gonzalo owned their own restaurant—they were still in college. Both were putting in lots of hours at their respective jobs.

"We're here for you," Mia said. "Dylan and I are here for you."

Sadie turned silent over that one—feeling happy and about to cry. She still wasn't sure if Mia liked her.

"You have plenty of time," Mia added. "Finish, por favor. Finish school."

She sucked up the tears and nodded.

"Now who can we put on the guest list?"

She was happy to name Alexis and Gillian. They would be her bridesmaids. She made Gillian maid of honor. "Oh, do you think Carmen would want to be a bridesmaid?" Mia nodded and wrote *Bridesmaid* next to Carmen's name.

"Now who should we invite from your side of the family?" Mia queried.

Of course, she wanted Felipe, Isabel, Constanza, Mateo, Luna, and Luciana, and their other children. She rounded out the list with three people from the yoga studio, plus four people from the college who did stuff with her and Gonzalo on occasion. Sterling was out.

"Don't you want to invite your aunt and uncle?"

Feeling stung by the question, she shook her head. Mia and Dylan must have been apprised of her situation on the island. She willed Mia to understand—to not press her on this one. But Mia held her gaze. "Sadie, this is an important ceremony. Your family should be there."

It hurt to shake her head more forcefully, but she did, thinking she wouldn't have minded having Leonard. He was her only living blood relative, as far as she knew. Maybe her biological father was still alive… But if he was, he'd never bothered with her. Leonard liked her all right, but Leonard liked Linny more. She never wanted to see Linny again. "No!"

She really wanted Bev and Nate to attend. As her thoughts reached back to happy times with the Bainbridge Island couple, Mia eyed her, "Sadie? Is there someone else you want to invite?"

She should have apologized for the money she took off the wall! She should have paid Bev back. She felt an impulse to tell Mia about Bev. She couldn't shake Bev. If it weren't for Bev… But she forced Bev into the recesses of her brain so she could ignore her. "That's it."

Sadie married Gonzalo beneath the sun shining down on a bluff above the sea. Felipe closed the restaurant to host the reception. That was his gift to them—what he and Isabel gave her and Gonzalo. All of Sadie's guests showed up. So did Gonzalo's guests, including Teresa and her family. That was a surprise. *Why did Mia have to invite her?* At first the whole thing burned. She didn't know Mia was going to invite Teresa! Mia should have warned her. She kept thinking about the situation, trying to be OK with it. She'd glance over at Teresa. Like she'd see her laughing with Carmen. *Well, they're definitely tight!* Then she'd see Teresa smiling at Dylan, who was chatting with Teresa's parents. *So Teresa's family matters to Gonzalo's family. I have to deal with this! Teresa's family will be around. Teresa's family is here and mine isn't! Teresa is so successful, and I…*

But then, the hours passed, and she forgot about Gonzalo's ex-wife. They began eating and dancing and talking and laughing.

At some point, Teresa came up to Sadie and Gonzalo to say, "I'm happy for you!' And Sadie could tell maybe Teresa meant it because she had not attended without her own date. Standing beside her was a professor. Jose.

Gonzalo's way cuter! She thought this as she looked him over. The professor was a short man with an easy smile, one that crinkled the lines around his eyes. She was still considering Jose's features when he winked at her, making her laugh—before Teresa whisked him away.

Everything was practically perfect, except for Bev. Her dearest friend (and boss) on the island had missed out on the fiesta. Bev had missed out on an entire week of fiestas!

From the very beginning, Gonzalo had figured out how to pry stuff out of her. Like how her mother had died—how her aunt had acted. Gonzalo knew her uncle ignored practically everything her aunt ever did. He knew Sadie didn't think she'd go to college. She'd told him about her lame guidance counselor. How it had been so horrible to see Hunter kissing that girl on Instagram. Her relationship with Sterling. But she'd never told him about Bev. She kept Bev wrapped so tight inside of her, nobody in Morro Bay knew she existed.

She needed to get over Bev because the celebration wasn't over.

They honeymooned in San Francisco, so beautiful and hilly with its fine water views—the bridge—better than any romance novel. This was the best her life had ever been. San Francisco was awesome! As Gonzalo showered in the hotel bathroom, she stood before the window studying skyscrapers, seagulls, and bits of the bay. She'd faced the hard part. She'd found her place in the world, which was Gonzalo's studio. She could enjoy her new marriage and this fabulous city!

The Next Hard Part

When she and Gonzalo returned to Morro Bay, things pretty much went back to normal. Except, her husband wouldn't let her split the rent. Though this decision bothered her, she let him have his way. She wanted poetry from her husband, not a fight. She and Gonzalo were becoming close in a way she'd never experienced with anyone. She wanted to give him everything, including her money. She insisted she had enough to pay her fair share, but he refused to accept it. The irony of this decision was that she was able to save even more money because she was no longer paying rent to Felipe and Isabel. She still had her bank account, and the money was piling up.

As the months passed, they talked—they worked together—they played—they had sex. Gonzalo read poetry out loud. She taught him a few yoga moves to help with stress. Yet when she had time to herself, she pretended to chat with Bev. She told Bev she would own a restaurant someday. She and Gonzalo. He was in his second to last semester—they still attended the college part-time. She nattered on to Bev about how, after Gonzalo earned his AS, he was going to start looking for commercial space. And Dylan, his father, planned to give them the down payment. She told Bev about how she'd tried to contribute financially. "I can help with that," she'd said. But Gonzalo just shook his head. "We've got plenty. Pop and I have plenty."

Still, the mysterious feeling stayed with her—the thing that linked her and Gonzalo. She felt the mysterious feeling growing big inside of her. When she told Gonzalo about it, he claimed he had it, too. The studio was tiny for two, but they didn't notice.

One morning, Sadie was home alone, working on a composition at their small table when the phone rang. She answered and recognized the sound of her husband's hysterical weeping.

"Gonzalo! What happened?"

"Pop's gone!"

Oh no! It was hard to understand everything he was saying through his sobs, but she managed to make out the words "heart attack" and "dead on arrival."

Their days turned bleak—stony quiet, and sad. Gonzalo took incompletes and stopped attending school. Mia worked in a floral shop, but she didn't earn enough to keep her and Carmen afloat. She certainly didn't earn enough for Carmen's tuition, though Gonzalo told his sister to stay in school. He told Sadie to stay in school. Sadie consented, but she continued working for Felipe.

"I can help with Carmen's tuition," she offered. But he brushed her away. Though a week later, he accepted her share of the rent. Sadie tried not to notice how this made him angry.

At the funeral, she felt like the lone gringa sitting in the church. A few other Anglos did attend. People from the college, plus some older family friends. As she sat listening to the service, she couldn't brush away the thought that this was someone else's family.

Gonzalo stopped reading poetry out loud to her. He accepted two shifts at his old restaurant in San Luis Obispo.

"You should return to college," she said on a rare evening when they were eating at home together.

"I can't afford it," he snarled.

"We can afford it." She got up to stack a pile of dishes on the kitchenette counter.

"Sadie…" He looked exasperated. He said, "Maybe we should move in with Mama and Carmen."

The thought of having Mia's eyes on her at all times made her insides buck. "We need our privacy." She didn't want to live with a woman who continued to fantasize about a marriage that was dead. She was pretty sure Gonzalo had no interest in going back to Teresa, but… And while Mia seemed to like her all right, Gonzalo was her pride and joy. Gonzalo was too old to be living with his mother! "If you'd just accept…" But she decided not to finish what she was about to say, because he wasn't listening.

Felipe's family had generously given her the room she'd needed to discover her adult life. Now she wanted to give back, to share what she'd earned over the years. Her stash was nice and fat.

"I'm just saying…" Gonzalo said.

She stood behind his chair and put her arms around him. "I have seed money. Let's open our restaurant!"

"I'm not going to allow my wife to support me," he yelled, jerking out of her embrace as he stood.

"What the?" She stared at him hard. "This is why you won't let me help? Gonzalo, I have money. I've been saving for years. If we started the restaurant…"

His shoulders stiffened. "I've got to make sure Carmen stays in school. That was Pop's dream."

"Of course," she replied. She stroked his arm before he moved it away.

Dylan had been focused on getting Carmen to the graduation ceremony. Dylan kept saying this—around everybody. Sadie had found this cool—the way Dylan wanted his daughter to succeed at Cal Poly. His pride in her was touching.

"He was so excited about her finishing," Gonzalo declared.

She pointed at her chest. "I'm becoming an accountant. If you would just let me sit down with all the figures…"

"No!"

"You're being an ass!"

"Is that what you think of me?" he shouted. His glare was fierce as they stood staring each other down like male elephant seals. She was sure their weird noses would have flopped in threatening ways—if they'd had weird noses.

Gonzalo walked out the door.

A few hours later, she received a phone call. "I'm staying with Mama."

A blast of hurt blew through her. "Do you want me to…"

"No!"

He stayed away for three nights. During that time, he refused to communicate. She finally called Mia for her own support, and her mother-in-law cooed, "He needs to be with us right now. His father's death is so raw inside of him. Try to understand."

She did try, but she wished it was her he needed and not them. She wished Gonzalo had turned to her.

Heaviness settled into her limbs, her torso, and even yoga did not shoo it away. She would smile at the customers in Felipe's restaurant, as if she could will things to be all right.

"Be patient," Felipe whispered.

At home, she kept their studio tidy. She did her homework. She remained terrified Gonzalo would not stay. They hadn't been together long enough for the relationship to root deep down into Morro Bay. He'd already divorced one woman, so… She felt disposable. At least she had the job at Felipe's. She'd be the one who'd have to move, because this was really his place. She'd have to start all over again! The little room at Felipe's had been taken by the new waiter.

When Gonzalo finally inched his way through the front door, he looked chagrined. He studied her face, not smiling—but he was not so angry now.

She didn't let him get away with this. She stood up strong!

"Sadie…"

"We need to talk," she said. She'd been thinking about what she needed to say for three whole days.

"That's what Mama said," he sighed, scrutinizing her face even more carefully.

"Gonzalo, we are a team. A team!"

When he didn't respond, she pushed harder. "We could make this restaurant work if you would get over yourself."

"Just hear me out," he said.

"No, you hear me out!" It was time, she thought. It was time to introduce him to Bev.

She proceeded to tell him how Bev and Nate had been the best team.

"Bev and Nate?"

She backed up and gave him the whole story—how she'd gotten started with Bev and Nate—and how they ran a popular restaurant on the island—how they made everything work by working together. Bev and Nate were living a good life.

"It's the money, Sadie."

"I have over a $100,000!" she exclaimed.

He looked at her funny. Then he really looked at her.

"I've been saving since high school."

"I don't want my wife…" She'd come to see how he became slightly hysterical whenever he thought a woman was taking charge.

Gently, she touched his arm. "We're a team," she insisted.

"It's just that…" He waved his arm at some invisible place.

"You contribute so much, Gonzalo. You really do."

He crumbled then, beginning to weep, and she wrapped her arms around him, feeling better because he wanted her to hold him. "You need to cry over your Pop. He was a wonderful man."

They remained quiet for a long time. After a while, he said, "He wasn't always so wonderful." When she searched his expression, he continued. "Pop wanted me to be like him. I wasn't. I knew I wasn't. I couldn't pound a nail straight, but he wanted me to learn so I could join the family business. Now I can't take it over because I'm not good enough." His face was scrunched and twisted.

"You're good at other things," she whispered. "And we will have our own family business."

"Pop was so impressed by Teresa. 'Cal Poly,' he used to say. Then Pop started wondering if Carmen could get in. He egged her on. He encouraged her. He never talked like that over my dreams. He just complained I didn't know how to hold two boards together. He grumbled about how I couldn't keep things straight with Teresa."

"Do you wish you'd stayed together? With Teresa?" She wasn't sure it was the right time to probe with the question that had been plaguing her since day one, but she couldn't stop herself. She'd become obsessed over the idea he regretted his divorce. She worried he viewed her as second best.

"At first, I did." He said this cautiously, peeping at her. "Eventually, I had to admit we didn't have much in common. We both like to write. Yes. But then she became interested in history. She kept talking about her classes—all the other stuff she was doing at Cal Poly. I was interested in going to a good cooking school, but

Cal Poly was eating up everything in our home. I mean, Teresa was into it."

"It is expensive," she agreed.

"I could have made it at Cal Poly."

"That's obvious, Gonzalo!" she proclaimed, as a realization over what was really going on sank in. "Your writing is gorgeous. You can transfer to Cal Poly."

"Not now." He sounded defeated.

But she put her index finger to his lips. "Not now is right. Because we will discuss this later."

He held on to her and they snuggled a while. They made love for the first time since his father died. When they were cuddling once more, he caught her eye. "$100,000! Wow-wee, Sadie. I knew you were the woman for me. I'm proud of you, Baby. I really am."

"If you'd just let me be the accountant I am finally becoming, we could earn even more."

His physical being was softer now, and he appeared to be listening, but she didn't push. She would get the details out of him on another day. She would find out how much his mother made. What Carmen's tuition was. How much he was earning as a chef. How much rents were. What they needed for seed money. What sort of loans might be possible. Financial aid for Carmen. She would gather every detail and figure out how they could make their lives work, so they could thrive. She hoped Mia wouldn't mind.

The mess between them melted, with one exception. Gonzalo wanted to move back to his childhood home. "Mama needs us." He said this one night as they lay in bed together.

She sat up and switched on the lamp next to her side of the bed. She propped her pillow against the headboard. "You mean she needs you."

"Sadie..."

"Gonzalo, we've got to talk about this."

He was propping up his pillow when he answered, "Yes, we do!"

Another elephant seal showdown, she thought.

"We need our privacy!"

"We'll have privacy. That house is huge compared to this." He motioned at the dresser just inches away.

She could just picture it. She and Gonazalo trying to make love as Carmen or Mia walked past their bedroom door. No thank you!

"That house is paid for! But it's a fair amount of work—the yards and stuff. We could save money and help my family."

She hated to be the party pooper, the one who was getting in the way of Vargas family bliss. Though she was a Vargas now. But she didn't feel like one.

When she'd announced her impending nuptials to Alexis and Gillian, Alexis asked if she planned to keep her last name. "A lot of women are doing that these days," Gillian nodded supportively.

"Naw." She shook her head. "My last name doesn't mean anything to me. Neither does my father."

She was a Vargas, but that was Mia's house.

"Just think about it. OK?" He kissed her to sweeten the deal, and she relaxed with him down, down beneath the covers.

A week later, Mia left a message on her phone while Sadie was at work, a move Mia had never made before.

Sadie, could we get together soon? There's something I want to discuss.

She called her right back. "What's up?"

"It's best if we talk in person. Would you meet me at the house at 10 am tomorrow? It's your morning off, isn't it?" Mia knew everything about their lives.

When she arrived at the Vargas place the following day, her mother-in-law showed her to the family room before asking about her drink preference.

"Coffee would be good. Nothing to eat, though," she added, holding up one hand.

Mia returned, carrying a tray with two orange Fiestaware mugs of coffee, plus cream and sugar. She placed the tray on the coffee table and smiled. "Please," she said, gesturing at the cup closest to Sadie.

"Thanks!" she said brightly.

Sadie doctored her coffee as Mia did the same. They stirred the hot fragrant liquid in unison, both silent. Sadie took a sip. "Mmm. This is delicious, Mia." The brew was spicy.

Her mother-in-law leaned back into the maroon armchair she'd claimed. "It's an old family recipe," she responded, before eyeing Sadie, as if calculating something. "How's school going? You're almost finished. Sí?"

She gave her mother-in-law the overview of the last classes she needed to knock out before she had her degree. "I sure wish Gonzalo would go back to school."

Mia leaned forward. "Gonzalo worries about us."

"Once I'm an accountant, I can bring in more money."

"That sounds like an excellent plan, mija." Mia took a sip of her coffee. "But right now…" She waved one arm around the room. "We have all this space. And…"

"Oh, but we need…"

"Hear me out, child."

She braced herself, feeling the roots beneath this home claiming her ankles like thick vines.

"You know I have a studio in the backyard?"

She could see where the line of this conversation was headed. Her smile felt forced. "It's very nice, Mia."

"I've asked Teresa's father to expand the space so it can be converted into a true apartment. A what do you call them? A mother-in-law." Her expression turned wry.

"Our studio suits us!"

"Sadie." Mia said her name gently. "I will live in the studio in the backyard. You and Gonzalo will run this larger home. It's getting too big for me."

"But Carmen…"

"Carmen plans to attend graduate school at UCLA. We'll keep her room in shape for her, of course."

"But…"

"If you agree to this plan, you'll strengthen the bond between you and Gonzalo." She tapped at her own breast. "Dylan and I… We worked hard to have our dream home. It's been a wonderful dream. We've been happy here." Her voice caught and sputtered. Sadie tried not to stare at her grief. "But the property taxes are shooting through the roof… And I… I can't stay here if you and Gonzalo don't help."

Sadie looked over the walls painted in ocher, rust, and tan. They were decorated with photos and a few landscape paintings, one with an orchard in full bloom. The matching maroon sofa she rested on was comfy. The home had been loved. This living room set beckoned a warm family to sit together around the coffee table.

"Please don't make me beg, daughter-in-law…"

Sadie shook her head, "Mia… I…" But then she thought about Gillian and the home she would someday inherit. For now, Gillian couldn't afford an apartment. And Alexis had gotten help on her little cottage. Well, Sadie had made her own money. But it wasn't enough for a house and a small business…

"You will have your privacy." Mia said this firmly.

Aghast, she stared at her mother-in-law. "Did Gonzalo…"

"Pero no, mija. He didn't need to tell me how you want privacy." She nodded conspiratorially. "A woman knows."

"Um. Well, sure."

"Do we have an agreement?"

The decision was clearly not hers, and this nagged at her. "What does Gonzalo say?"

"What do you think, daughter-in-law? He wants to be the head of his childhood home, place of his corazón."

But what about my heart?

Mia toasted Sadie with her cup. "We have much to discuss. The restaurant…"

"He's afraid to start one," Sadie admitted.

"I can help you. Both of you," she added quickly. "I ran Dylan's business for years." Her mother-in-law's expression was a measuring stick. "I kept his books shipshape."

"But I wanted…"

"Have you ever run a business, daughter-in-law?"

"Well, no."

Her mother-in-law's eyes sharpened as they drilled into hers. "I can help you learn how to keep Gonzalo's books."

"But my degree…"

"You will earn your degree. Why not? But first things first."

"Cal Poly?"

Mia threw up her hands, but she laughed. "You young people… And Cal Poly!"

Moving

It took Teresa's father and two helpers a month to transform Mia's studio into a one-bedroom apartment complete with kitchenette and a full bathroom. He cut a wide rectangle into one side and added French doors that opened onto a small deck where Mia began tending to a variety of potted plants. Mia bought her own cute patio set, though a much larger one already accompanied the big house, as they started calling the place.

Sadie and Gonzalo moved in a month later, settling into the master bedroom which thankfully came with a decent master bathroom no one else felt the need to use. Carmen was rarely home. Though Teresa came over on occasion to help Carmen with her homework, a complex dynamic Sadie couldn't wait to get rid of when Carmen finally headed to UCLA.

Still, it felt—almost—as if she and Gonzalo were brand new homeowners, though there was no way in hell they could have afforded this place, now valued at 1.5 million dollars. There was no way they could have afforded the furniture in this place.

Gonzalo was already joking about trying to keep up with the property taxes, but this did not make Sadie laugh. Their two incomes, as well as the money Mia made at the flower shop was enough to give them breathing room. But Mia was already egging Gonzalo on over starting the restaurant, a job that had once fallen to Sadie.

"We've got many secret recipes in this family," Mia reminded him one Sunday afternoon after they'd all sat down to a large midday meal. Sunday was the day they usually did this, though Sadie had noticed how Mia was managing to find her way into other meals during the week. "You know we can give Felipe a run for his money."

Gonzalo smirked, while Sadie looked from one Vargas to the other. Looked like those two were becoming a team.

"You've already taught me how to make most of your fine recipes, Mama. Maybe you can teach Sadie…"

"Sadie wants to do the books," Mia shot back. "I will teach her bookkeeping."

"Well, you're a pro at that. Pop was sure proud of your business acumen."

Mia smiled at her son weakly, almost too humbly, but Sadie could tell she loved the compliment. Why was Sadie even bothering to earn her degree in Business with a certificate in Accounting? She pushed back her chair. "I've got to get ready for work."

"I thought you didn't work on Sunday," Mia said.

"Normally no, but someone is sick. Felipe just called about it."

"I forgot to mention it, Mama," Gonzalo cut in. "Sadie never misses a chance to earn more money. She…"

"When are you two going to look for a commercial space?"

"Soon," Gonzalo said. "Right, Sadie?"

"Sure."

She was still fuming when she started her shift at Felipe's. She forced her good customer service tone to mask this anger. "Even if the sky is falling around your personal life, you need to put on your beautiful smile and make the customer feel at home," Bev told her. Sadie figured she was pulling off her usual charm. But during a lull in their regular bustling, Felipe tapped her on the shoulder. "What's eating you?"

"Nothing," she replied, becoming hyperaware of the clanking dishes.

"Duckling?"

"It's her house!"

"Yes it is, Duckling." He placed his hands gently on either side of her face. "And she is grieving."

"I know, but…"

"You've experienced loss, and so has she. Now give her a break."

"But the restaurant…"

"I'd hire Mia in a heartbeat."

So would Bev, she finally admitted to herself. Bev wouldn't blow this one.

Late that evening, when she finally had Gonzalo to herself, they sat in the family room, sipping wine. She raised her glass and pronounced, "Let's find our restaurant!"

"I was about to make the same suggestion."

They did tend to be in sync, her and Gonzalo. She was lucky. "We'll need a loan officer," she pointed out.

"You're right," he smiled.

"Shouldn't we get preapproved?"

"You think of everything, Sadie." As she took a sip of wine, he motioned her over, "C'mere."

The Restaurant

They found their loan officer. They found their realtor. They found a commercial space, which Sadie didn't completely love, but it was all they could afford. It was an older home in the northern part of town. The house had been converted into a restaurant long ago. As she sat with Gonzalo and the loan officer for the purpose of signing the papers, she felt twitchy. She reached for a breathing technique Alexis liked to use in the yoga class. Her stash was being poured into this humble building that would need some touching up. Her precious life raft was going into an unknown hole, and she didn't like the way this felt, even with a husband on hand to keep her stable. Even with the Vargas family home. Even with Mia's business acumen. Her money was the down payment. Meanwhile, a pile of Vargas family funds had been reserved for overhead and supplies. They planned to offer lunch and dinner. For now, no breakfast, so that she and Gonzalo could take classes in the morning.

Mia worked through the long list of expenses necessary to get them started. After she went back to the little house for the night, Sadie and Gonzalo discussed her ideas against what they'd been learning at school. There had been some updates since Dylan and Teresa's father began their contracting business all those years ago. They made their own to-do list, which they planned to go over with Mia on another day.

Mia taught Sadie how to use QuickBooks. She had to admit, her mother-in-law was saving them time. It would have taken her hours to learn what Mia could teach as they worked through the screens together.

"I will get us off the ground, Sadie. You can decide later if you want to take over the books," her mother-in-law said.

"Of course, I will!"

"Maybe you'll want to get that degree at Cal Poly…"

This line of discussion didn't feel like a duel. Not exactly. But she wasn't sure what Mia really wanted. Did her mother-in-law want Sadie to become a CPA and work with other people's finances? Or did she want her to assume full responsibility for the restaurant? Mia probably wanted her to have babies. She and Gonzalo were holding off on starting a family. She sure as hell wasn't going to talk about the ins and outs of birth control with her mother-in-law. Though she would have done with Bev. Maybe the restaurant would be enough. Or maybe… Her college advisor was still pushing her to transfer, which made her feel real proud.

When they were ready to open the restaurant, the Vargas family threw a fiesta with lots of free food, streamers, balloons, party favors, live music, and a piñata. Gonzalo, Sadie, Carmen, and Mia donned their favorite nice outfits, clothes they wouldn't normally work in. Not in a restaurant. But there would be a photographer on hand to document the moment for social media. Her husband roamed from table to table, joking and laughing. He knew most of the people in the room.

Mia stood next to Sadie at the register, which was a used piece of equipment they were in the process of fussing over, when the first customers of the afternoon, an older Latino couple, approached them. "Delicioso!" the gentleman said as he handed Sadie a fistful of cash. "Keep the change."

The bill on top was a dollar, though she could tell bigger bills lay beneath it. As she stared at it, a tear welled up.

"Sadie?" Mia queried.

"Oh, I'm just happy," she shot back. She handed the money to Mia, all but the dollar bill. Mia frowned momentarily as Sadie set the bill before her on the counter. She opened the catchall drawer to rummage until she spotted a blue felt pen, which she grabbed and uncapped.

"What are you doing, mija?"

She wrote, right across George Washington's face. "First One!"

Mia giggled as Sadie tacked it on the wall behind them. She decided then and there she wouldn't allow any other dollars to be pinned around the restaurant—just this one-dollar bill. Their first one. Yet the rest of the day, she couldn't help but feel sad.

This low-grade depression hovered as Sadie barreled into the restaurant business with everything she had. Everyone worked hard. Even Carmen helped whenever she could, though they'd hired a few part-time workers to make sure everything was covered. The customers kept coming through the door. They were getting good reviews on Yelp and TripAdvisor. Two local papers ran write-ups about the new eatery. *The sauces are especially unusual. The food, extra fresh.* Sadie smiled and nodded and did her job. Gonzalo was thrilled at how well things were going. They chewed over various details together as they drifted off to sleep at night.

Mia stopped coming into the big house as often. She seemed to understand they needed to chill out when they weren't working.

A month later, Sadie had the first morning to herself in she didn't know how long. She slept in, tired from the long hours. She lollygagged in bed the way she used to do when she lived in the small room provided by Felipe and Isabel. After she opened her eyes all the way, she got up to use the bathroom, and then she dove back under the covers to lay there some more. She left the blinds clamped down tight.

A couple of hours later, there was a knock on the door. "Sadie," Mia said softly. "Are you all right?"

"I'm fine," she said, feeling irritated, though she kept that customer service tone in her voice.

"Come and have coffee with me on my deck. It's a beautiful day."

"Oh, all right."

Mia did have this way of doing things with panache. Her mother-in-law had placed a vase filled with purple irises on the glass table. A white swirl thermal coffee carafe rested in the middle. There were two blue Fiestaware coffee mugs, the usual cream and sugar, and a plate of croissants, several of which contained chocolate.

"Good morning!" Mia smiled

She smiled back shyly as she mumbled, "Good morning." She was worried Mia would think she was being lazy.

"I'm glad you were able to get some much-needed rest."

Relief coursed through her. She appreciated Mia's sweetness. "It sure has been a whirlwind, hasn't it, Mia?"

Her mother-in-law poured coffee into the two mugs. "It may be too early to predict… I think we've got a restaurant."

"Yeah," Sadie sighed. They were doing good. She picked up one of the chocolate croissants and took a big bite. "Mmm. Do you know how to do any French cooking?"

"I've tried it a time or two."

She scrutinized her mother-in-law, who was still pretty with dark eyes and wavy brown hair that had been dyed. Mia was becoming settled looking. "You and Gonzalo," Sadie said. "You both love to cook. Must be in the genes."

"And you don't." This was not a question.

"Naw…" She shook her head.

"Something is bothering you, mija. Something is bothering you a lot."

They held each other's gaze as she felt her rebellious side kicking in. But she didn't want another elephant seal standoff.

"Mija?"

Sadie exhaled and said, "Bev."

"Gonzalo told me about your friends. They're running a restaurant on Bainbridge Island. Sí?"

"Yes. Bev and Nate. They're a team."

Her mother-in-law smiled. "And?" she probed. "Why didn't you invite them to the wedding?" Mia's gaze was firm.

"They were just my bosses."

"You know, Sadie… Felipe once said to me… He said, 'That Sadie was really well trained.' Felipe said he was surprised by how quickly you learned everything, winning the customer's hearts."

"Felipe said that?" The words hurt and felt good at the same time.

"This Bev and Nate. They were more than bosses. No?"

She felt something cutting free as she launched into the story about how her uncle loved her a little and how her aunt didn't love her at all. She told Mia about how Bev had given her a ticket off the island by training her to work in See Birds Diner. Bev had given her great experience, especially for someone her age. Bev had been a friend who'd trusted her and listened to her and then she'd gone and taken Bev's money off the wall.

"What do you mean?"

She breathed into words focused on how there were several thousand dollars tacked around the restaurant, which she'd always thought was funny and maybe crazy. She never needed any of it. Bev was paying her. But then her aunt started wanting more free help. So she came up with a plan to get out of there. But then Linny went and stole her debit card. Maybe Linny guessed she wanted to leave. Sadie already had her ticket. She'd packed her backpack. Everything was supposed to work out, but she couldn't get a new debit card. So she helped herself. She betrayed her best friend. And she hadn't been able to make things right. She didn't know how, even now, when they were doing so well, and everything was good in Morro Bay. How did she apologize and explain? "Mia, you must think I'm a little thief."

"No, daughter-in-law…"

"I'm just like my mother."

Mia shook her head more vigorously. She didn't think that. "You were young, and you were scared. And your aunt, well…"

"She didn't like me!"

Mia grabbed ahold of her hand. "But you've proven yourself. In many ways. And you don't need to hold onto all of that guilt."

"But what about Bev?"

"Sadie… You are smart, and you are thoughtful, and you are a good planner. You will figure something out."

"Maybe."

"I think you will."

The next time she had a morning to herself, she headed to her bank to withdraw a pile of dollar bills. This was her own money from her own bank account. She and Gonzalo had others. She raced home and zoomed into the smaller bedroom they'd converted into a home office. Her gaze darted wildly around the room till she spotted a fuchsia felt pen in a canister. *Perfect.* Like a student held after school, she proceeded to write: *Love, Sadie.* 500 times. She bundled these bills tightly. She packed them up and wrapped them with a whole lot of tape. The next day she mailed the package to Bev. That and a picture of her and Gonzalo with Mia and Carmen. Everyone posing with broad smiles in front of The Mole Café.

Kari Wergeland, who hails from Davis, California, is a librarian and writer. She moved to Oregon at the age of 14 and eventually attended the University of Oregon, where she earned a BA in English. She holds an MLS in Librarianship from the University of Washington and an MFA in Creative Writing with an emphasis in poetry from Pacific University. Her work has appeared many journals, including *Catamaran Literary Reader, Jabberwock Review,* and *New Millennium Writings.* She once served as children's book reviewer for *The Seattle Times.* In 2019, her chapbook, *Breast Cancer: A Poem in Five Acts* (Finishing Line Press) was named an Eric Hoffer Book Award finalist in the chapbook category. Meanwhile, her long library career has taken her into libraries up and down the West Coast. More recently, she's returned to her hometown to work as an adjunct librarian for the Los Rios Community College District.